Euphoric that she had the freedom to touch and feel him, she pushed her fears aside and gave in to her desires.

They came together in an explosion of need that rocked her world.

"You don't know what meeting you has done to me." Luca kissed every inch of her face and throat. "I could eat you alive. Don't ask me to stop because I can't, *bellissima*."

"I don't want you to stop. Surely you know that by now. Why else do I keep finding excuses to stay?"

"I love you, Gabriella Parisi. I'm so in love with you, I can't think about anything else. Don't say it's too soon, or that we barely know each other. None of that matters because we know how we feel."

Dear Reader,

My Christmas story has been a delight to write because it touches on the heart-wrenching theme about children who need special blessings in their lives. The heroine in this story has been the recipient of a special blessing and is in a position to bring happiness to deserving, adorable children everywhere.

The idea for this book came because of the following story. My son and my granddaughter were flying to Denver, Colorado, from Salt Lake City, Utah. Before they got off the jet, the pilot heard my granddaughter say she wished she could sit in his seat in the cockpit. To their surprise, the pilot granted her that wish and gave her the thrill of her life. He put his hat on her head and took a picture of the two of them.

I started thinking about all the deserving children who could use a once-in-a-lifetime thrill to make them happy. I looked at my son in the picture. He's an alpine skier in the Colorado mountains and is already teaching my darling granddaughter to become a downhill skier. My mind started to put a story together. But this one takes place in the Italian Dolomites. A boy and his parents are out enjoying a day of skiing, as carefree as my son and granddaughter were on that trip. But something unexpected occurs. I hope you'll read the story for a Christmas treat and find out what happens to this very special family.

Enjoy!

Rebecca

The Magnate's Holiday Proposal

Rebecca Winters

ISBN-13: 978-0-373-74461-9

The Magnate's Holiday Proposal

First North American Publication 2017

This edition published by arrangement with Harlequin Books S.A.

For questions and comments about the quality of this book, please contact us at CustomerService@Harlequin.com.

Printed in U.S.A.

Rebecca Winters lives in Salt Lake City, Utah. With canyons and high alpine meadows full of wildflowers, she never runs out of places to explore. They, plus her favorite vacation spots in Europe, often end up as backgrounds for her romance novels—because writing is her passion, along with her family and church. Rebecca loves to hear from readers. If you wish to email her, please visit her website at cleanromances.com.

Books by Rebecca Winters

Harlequin Romance

The Billionaire's Club

Return of Her Italian Duke
Bound to Her Greek Billionaire
Whisked Away by Her Sicilian Boss

The Vineyards of Calanetti

His Princess of Convenience

The Montanari Marriages

The Billionaire's Baby Swap
The Billionaire Who Saw Her Beauty

Greek Billionaires

The Millionaire's True Worth
A Wedding for the Greek Tycoon

The Billionaire's Prize

Visit the Author Profile page
at Harlequin.com for more titles.

Praise for Rebecca Winters

"Readers will be swept away... Winters' fine romance unfolds at the perfect pace, so one can digest the relationship and still enjoy the antics of being a billionaire."

—*RT Book Reviews* on *The Billionaire Who Saw Her Beauty*

CHAPTER ONE

November, two years earlier.
Piancavallo, the Italian Dolomites, Italy

"PAPÀ? IS THIS where you skied when you were my age?"

"Yes. I'd practice right here whenever my parents would let me."

"I want to be an Olympic champion like you."

"I have no doubts you will be one day, Dino," his *mamma* said. "But it's getting cold and time to go back to our chalet. We'll come again tomorrow, darling."

"Urra!"

Suddenly the three of them heard a loud crack higher up the mountain.

"What was that, Papà?"

"We have to get off the mountain, *now*!"

November 29, present day

On Thursday morning Luca Berettini left his villa for work later than usual and got in the car to drive to Spilimbergo in Northeast Italy. It took only a few minutes from Luca's home in Maniago, Italy, eleven miles away.

For the last year and a half, Luca had been acting CEO of Berettini Plastics, their hundred-year-old family business, while his father, Fabrizo Berettini, had been recovering from a heart attack. The position was one he'd never wanted or sought. But both the board and his mother had pressured him to do it. She'd done everything in the world for him all her life, and he couldn't turn her down.

Since the avalanche that had robbed Luca of his wife and Dino's mother, Luca had run a business of his own on the side, all to do with the manufacture of Italian skis and boots. His venture had proved lucrative. If the gods were kind, the day might come when Luca could say goodbye to the job of CEO and be fully involved with his interest in the ski industry.

The horrendous avalanche that had changed his world and had kept him away from the ski slopes hadn't altered his love for the sport.

What a joy it would be to walk away and have the freedom to do what he really wanted, but he couldn't do that until he knew the outcome of his father's health.

As for Dino, until Luca knew what kind of life was in store for his son after the impending operation to remove a benign brain tumor, it was difficult to think about anything else. The boy meant more to him than life itself.

Luca parked his car and nodded to several of the employees before taking the private elevator to his suite on the third floor. As he entered, his secretary, Sofia, got up from her desk and hurried over to him. Something was going on. In a hushed voice she said, "Before you go in, I wanted to warn you that your father is here. He's been waiting several hours for you."

Anger swamped Luca. The doctor had ordered his father to stay home and continue to work with his various therapists until he was given permission to put in part-time work again. But that hadn't stopped him from crossing the threshold today. It was so like him to intrude on Luca's private life without warning. In the past he'd tried to sabotage several of Luca's relationships with women by making demands and criticisms.

Today was all Luca needed after having to console Dino following one of his nightmares this morning, but he knew exactly why his father had shown up and shouldn't have been surprised. When he hadn't gotten satisfaction after a fiery exchange on the phone with Luca last night, he'd decided to barge in on him.

Being armed with that information, Luca thanked Sofia for the heads-up and walked in his inner sanctum. His silver-haired sixty-eight-year-old father sat at the large oak desk while he read some sensitive documents Luca had been working on.

He looked at Luca without getting up. "I asked Sofia to hold your calls so I could talk to you."

How like his father to come to the office without advance warning when the doctor hadn't given him permission to be at work yet. Throughout Luca's life his father had interfered, never approving of his sporting interests, always trying to stifle his career ambitions that had nothing to do with the family plastics business. No girl, no woman was good enough for

Luca except the one they were fighting about right now.

"We said all there was to say last night on the phone."

His father slammed one hand on the desk. "I don't know why you continue to thwart me about Giselle."

"Frankly, I'll never understand why you hoped she and I would ever get together. I was never interested in her, which is why I married Catarina."

"But your wife has been dead for two years. Giselle is still very much alive and beautiful. Her father tells me it was you she always wanted. We're determined to get the two of you together. I told him I'd arrange it."

Luca shook his head. "Don't you understand I have more important things to think about at the moment? I'm dealing with my son's fears over his operation," he exploded. "Henri Fournier may be your best friend and the two of you are desperate to keep the fortunes of both our families sealed with a marriage, but I made it clear last night. I don't want to see his daughter and have no interest in any woman! Since you look settled in that chair where you once sat for years ruling the company, I'll leave it to you."

The older man's cheeks grew ruddy. He would never change. His father had been the same intransigent dictator for as long as Luca could remember. Nothing Luca had ever wanted or done had met with his father's approval, and Luca had given up hope for a transformation.

"Where are you going?"

"Home."

"Wait, Luca—"

But he walked back out and told Sofia to ring him if anything vital came up. Now would be a good time to do an on-site visit to the ski manufacturing plant he owned in nearby Tauriano before returning to Maniago. It might cool down his anger.

At three thirty that afternoon Luca returned home and found his son still in his pajamas watching TV in the family room.

"Hey—*piccolo*." He hugged him. "What's going on?"

"My favorite show."

Ines, the nanny, got up from the sofa and walked over to him. "It's the *Start with a Wish* program that's on every weekday afternoon."

Luca had heard of it. "He's obsessed with it because they make a child's wish come true."

If only that were really possible.

"I take it his headache finally passed."

"Yes."

Every headache his son suffered caused Luca pain that crossed over the older lines of grief etched on his hard-boned features. "After we have dinner, I'll take him to watch a hockey game. Hopefully it will get his mind off the operation."

He left the kitchen and raced up the stairs, as ever feeling devastated by Dino's condition. Earlier that morning his son had cried to him. "I dreamed I was in the avalanche and couldn't find Mamma. I wish she didn't have to die."

How many times had Luca heard that? He'd kissed the top of his head. "We all wish she were here, but at least we have each other, don't we?"

"Yes," his boy whispered.

"Pretty soon you're not going to have headaches anymore."

"But I'm scared."

"I know, but the operation is going to take them away. Doesn't that make you happy?"

"Yes, but what if I never wake up?"

Luca clutched him harder. "Where did you get an idea like that?"

"On TV."

"What show?"

"That cartoon, *Angel's Friends*. Raf's mother never woke up."

Diavolo. A simple cartoon had played on his fears, doing more damage. "Listen to me, Dino. I've had four operations in my life, and I'm just fine."

"Was Nonna with you?"

He'd closed his eyes, praying for inspiration. "Yes." Luca's mother had always been there for him. "And *I'll* be with you. Don't you know I wouldn't let anything happen to you?"

"Yes." But Dino's voice was muffled against Luca's shoulder and he'd finally fallen asleep.

The heavy lids that covered blue eyes revealed his misery. In the last year, his headaches had grown more frequent as the doctor said they would. When the medication didn't stop them, sleep was the only thing that seemed to help, but that meant he stayed in bed until they subsided.

At his last checkup three months ago, the doctor had brought up the operation to remove it. But Dino fought the very thought of one, even if it would make him feel better.

Now Luca was frightened, too, because the neurosurgeon told him the tumor was in a dangerous place. Removing it wasn't without risk. But Luca knew it had to be done so his son could be relieved of pain.

His operation had been scheduled for December 21, less than a month away now. Dr. Meuller, the Swiss-born doctor from Zurich who was doing some voluntary work in Africa, would fly in to the hospital in Padova to perform the surgery. Luca had arranged his business affairs so he'd be free during that time.

Luca and his mother had done everything to reassure Dino they'd be there for him during the surgery, but whenever it was mentioned, he would run to his room and sob. He wanted his mother, and no one could replace her. It broke his heart that Dino dreaded it so much.

Something out of the ordinary had to happen to help his son. Luca wished to heaven he knew what it was…

Another Monday.

Gabi Parisi left the house in Limena and drove the four miles under an overcast sky to the office of the Start with a Wish foundation in Padova, Italy. In the fifty-six-degree temperature, she didn't need a coat to wear over her long-sleeved blue sweater and black wool skirt.

After the weekend, Mondays meant tons of mail. So many letters came in from children needing help. Some required money for medical procedures or operations that parents or guardians couldn't provide. Others were dying and the family or caregivers wanted to grant them their greatest wish, which was beyond their means.

Edda Romano, Gabi's boss, was a famous philanthropist who had been giving away her money for worthy causes ever since her husband's untimely death. Being the heiress of the Romano manufacturing fortune had allowed her to establish the foundation that would continue to give happiness to children for generations. There was no one Gabi admired more than Edda. She felt it a privilege to work for this remarkable seventy-five-year-old woman who was truly selfless.

Gabi maneuvered through the heavy traffic and drove around the back of the building to the private parking area. After touching up her lipstick, she ran a brush through tousled ash-blond hair and got out of the car. To her surprise she was met with several wolf whistles coming from some workmen doing renovations on the building to the west.

Men.

Her divorce two years ago had put her off getting involved again. She'd moved back home with her widowed mother, who still worked part-time at the hospital as a pediatric nurse.

Gabi had gotten her college degree in accounting and had worked in a bank. She'd even fallen in love and had married the bank manager, having faith in a wonderful future. But a miscarriage soon after their marriage had been devastating. And then she'd learned her husband had been having an affair.

In less than a year of being married, it was over and she'd filed for divorce. Once again she'd started looking for another job.

When the position with Edda had opened up, Gabi had grabbed at it, sensing it would be a healing kind of work. Edda's whole purpose was to make children happy. Still mourning the baby she'd lost at five weeks, Gabi could pour out her love on other people's children.

The foundation business filled three floors of the neoclassic building, depending on the department where you were assigned. To Gabi's mind, she had the best position. She, along with four other women, had the exciting opportunity of opening and reading the letters. When they'd made their group decision about each child's letter, they took it to Edda in the suite next door to make the final decisions about what to do.

Once Gabi had gone inside the rear entrance and had grabbed a cup of coffee in the open reception room, she walked upstairs to the conference room on the second floor to get started for the day. She and her coworkers sat around a big oval table. Three of them were married, one was single and Gabi was divorced.

Stefania, the woman Edda had put in charge of their group, received the mail from the mail room and passed around the new letters that came in every day. Gabi marveled that so many children needed special help and praised Edda for the service she rendered on a continual basis. Such goodness put her in the category of a saint.

"*Buongiorno*," she said to Angelina and Clara, who'd already arrived. In a minute Stefania came in with Luisa, the one who still wasn't married and had become a good friend of Gabi's. They smiled at each other before Luisa sat down next to her. "How was your weekend?" she whispered to her friend.

"I spent it with my cousin. We did a lot of early Christmas shopping. What about you, Gabi?"

"My mother and I drove to Venice for the fun of it." Gabi had done a little sketching.

"How wonderful!"

Pretty soon everyone had settled down. Stefania opened the mailbag and distributed a bundle to each of them. Gabi opened her envelopes and pulled out the letters. Then they each took a turn to read a letter. In the afternoon they would form a consensus of what to turn over to Edda for final consideration. All the letters came from children who were deserving of blessings.

Just before lunch Gabi picked up her last letter. Most of them had been written in cursive by an adult. This one had been printed by a youngster and there was no greeting.

"My name is Dino Berettini." She didn't know of another Berettini except the international Berettini plastics conglomerate near

Venice. The billion-dollar business helped keep the country afloat financially.

"I am seven years old. Every night I tell God I am afraid to have an operation because my *mamma* died and won't be with me. But if it will take away my headaches and make my *papà* happy again, I will do it. He is never happy and I love him more than anyone in the entire world."

The words *make my* papà *happy again* swam before Gabi's eyes. They took her back to her childhood when at the age of seven, her adored father was dying. She'd gone to the priest after Mass and begged him to ask God to make him better. The priest smiled kindly and told her she should ask God herself.

Hurt that he hadn't said he would do it, she still went home and said her prayers, begging God to save her *papà*. Within two days he rallied and got better. In Gabi's mind a miracle had happened.

Touched by the sweet, prayer-like missive from this boy, she was moved to tears.

"Gabi?"

She looked up. Everyone was staring at her, so she read them the letter.

"What else does the letter say?" Stefania asked her.

"There isn't anything else. This child wrote what was in his heart. Obviously an adult had to address the envelope and mail it to us, but I'm convinced no one helped him with the wording."

"I agree. Read it to us again."

Gabi looked at Stefania. "I don't think I can without breaking down."

"I'll do it." Luisa reached for it and read it aloud. After she'd finished, she said, "What a sweet little boy. But he hasn't asked for anything."

"Yes he has," Gabi murmured. "He wants the foundation to grant his wish not to be afraid for the operation that will help him feel better and make his father happy."

"But we can't do that," Clara exclaimed.

Stefania shook her head. "No. It's beyond our power, but this is one letter Edda has to read. Enjoy your lunch. I'll see you back here at one thirty."

They all got up and left the building. Luisa and Gabi walked around the corner to the trattoria where they usually ate. While they ate pasta and salad, Luisa asked her why the letter had touched her so deeply.

"I don't know exactly. A combination of things made me tear up. He mentioned losing his mother, and it reminded me of my miscarriage and how I would never raise my child. As I told you, Santos and I got pregnant on our honeymoon. But I lost it after carrying it five weeks, and nothing could comfort me."

Luisa eyed her compassionately. "I can only imagine how painful that would have been for you."

"That was over two years ago. But when I read Dino's words today, some of those feelings returned. Now *he's* the one suffering so terribly."

"The poor little thing has lost his mother. The pathos in that one line squeezed my heart."

"I know," Gabi murmured. "Especially the last line that said his father was never happy."

Luisa shook her head. "In the six months I've been working here, we've never had a letter like this one."

"I agree. Today I found myself wishing a miracle would happen for that boy. He wrote that letter as an act of faith because of Edda's program. The trouble is, she can give any child a tangible gift, but she can't move mountains."

"No." Luisa shook her head. "It needs a miracle."

"Do you remember me telling you about the time I wanted a miracle so my father wouldn't die? That did happen and he lived until three years ago when he finally passed away from heart failure. If only one could happen again for Dino..."

On that solemn note they left to walk back to work. A half hour later Stefania told Gabi to go in Edda's office. Since Gabi had been the one who'd opened the letter and had been affected by it, their boss wanted to talk it over with her.

Gabi and Luisa exchanged surprised glances before she walked down the hall and entered Edda's private domain. The trim, classily dressed philanthropist with titian-colored hair smiled at Gabi and asked her to sit down opposite her desk. She held the letter in her hand.

"Stefania told me about your reaction while you were reading this. I confess tears welled up in my throat, too. That adorable child's simple plea for help leaves us with a dilemma."

"Luisa and I were talking about that over lunch. How do you move a mountain?"

"Exactly." She picked up the envelope the letter had come in. "Someone mailed it from Maniago. I did research while you were at lunch. There are two Berettini families living in that town. Does the name Luca Berettini mean anything to you?"

"No, but I immediately thought of the Berettini Plastics Company near Venice."

She nodded. "It's the family business. Recently the elder Berettini stepped down as head and now Luca Berettini, his son, has been made CEO. Dino is his boy."

"How do you know that?"

"Because of a tragedy that happened to that family two years ago. It was all over the media and in the newspaper. You didn't hear about it or see it on TV?"

Gabi lowered her head. "That was a difficult time for me and I'm afraid I hadn't been paying much attention to the news."

It was two years ago that Gabi had discovered her husband had been unfaithful to her. She'd already had a miscarriage. With her marriage in shambles, she'd filed for divorce. It had been a horrific time for her and she'd been blinded to anything going on around her at the time.

"I'm sorry to hear that. You've been a wonderful employee."

"Thank you. I've been so much better since you hired me to come to work for you. It's so marvelous making children happy. I'm more grateful to you for this job than you could possibly know."

"I'm glad of it."

"Please tell me what happened to Dino."

"Luca Berettini was a downhill alpine skier who became a gold medalist in the Olympics in his early twenties."

"I remember something about that. I was probably around sixteen at the time," Gabi murmured. "But that was ten years ago. I haven't heard anything about him since."

"You wouldn't have. He could have gone on for more medals but was taken into the family business early because of his brilliant marketing acumen. He married, and he and his wife had a son. Two years ago the three of them were skiing near their chalet in Piancavallo when they were caught in an avalanche."

"Oh, no—"

"I don't recall the details, but his wife was killed. According to all the reports, Luca saved his son from certain death."

"The boy would have been five then. Old enough to have memories of his mother."

"Yes. According to this letter, he needs some kind of an operation to cure his headaches."

Gabi's head lifted. "But he's afraid because he wants his mother with him."

"Sadly no one can bring her back, and they don't need money for an operation. Our foundation can't help him, but I'll get you the unlisted phone numbers of the Berettini families, hopefully before the day is out. When I do, why don't you try to reach the person who mailed Dino's letter and set up a time to visit him? He needs a personal visit to know we received it."

"I think that would be wonderful."

"Would you like to be the one to go from our office?"

"I'd love to be the one to visit him. I know what it's like to want a wish to come true."

Gabi was reminded of another experience at Christmastime around twelve years of age. One of her best friends had almost died from a bad appendix. Their group of friends were so sad, and someone suggested they wish on a star for her so she'd get better.

None of them really believed it would do

any good, but they'd grasped at any hope to pull their friend through. Wonder of wonders, she did recover. To Gabi it had been another miracle. This boy needed one, too.

"Good. However, the family may not allow it. But if they do, you can take him a gift to let him know we received his letter. Since it's getting close to Christmas, I'm thinking the latest building blocks game. It's a Christmas scene with trees and snowmen. Children that age love it. I'll ask our gift department to get it ready for him. But if it turns out the family doesn't want anyone to come, then we'll send him the gift."

"I knew you'd have a solution. You always do. Thank you for giving me this opportunity."

Gabi left her office and rejoined the others in the conference room. She told them what Edda had said. Near the end of the day Edda's secretary walked in and gave Gabi a sheet of paper with the telephone numbers of the Berettini families.

Stefania smiled at her. "Go ahead and make your call at the desk while we finish up."

"Thanks." She walked over to the corner of the room and sat down, wondering which number to choose first. But it didn't matter as long as she reached the person who sent the letter.

On the first call she was asked to leave a message. Gabi decided not to do that before trying the other number. On the third ring, someone picked up.

"Pronto?"

"Hello. My name is Signora Parisi. I'm calling from the Start with a Wish foundation in Padova. Today we received a letter from a boy named Dino Berettini. There was no address on the envelope, but we saw that it was postmarked from Maniago. Edda Romano, the founder, has asked me to speak to the person who knows about it."

Maybe Dino mailed it himself and no one in his family knew about it. If he'd wanted to keep it a secret, it was too late now.

"Signora Parisi? I'm Giustina Berettini, Dino's grandmother, the one who sent it for him." Her answer filled Gabi with relief. "I'm surprised you received it so quickly. I only mailed it on Friday."

"We try to be prompt with a reply when the letters come in because we know the desperate needs of these children."

"I was home with him on Friday when he said he wanted to watch your program," the older woman said. "I'd heard of the foundation, of course, but I'd never seen it on TV. Before long he asked me to help him with his letter and mail it. What he printed came straight from his heart."

Gabi nodded. "When I read the letter to my coworkers, we were all very touched. Once Edda read it, she suggested I contact your family. We realize he needs an operation, and we can't bring back his mother, but would it be possible for me to come and bring him a gift? Edda wants him to know all our prayers will be with him."

"That's very kind of you. He'll be so thrilled."

It would be a thrill for Gabi, too. "I'll bring it when it's the best time for you. I believe the sooner he receives it, the better."

"Would it be possible for you to come to my house in the morning? Say nine o'clock? Or is that too early? I don't have any idea about your hours of work."

"Nine o'clock would be no problem. What's the address?"

After writing it down, Gabi hung up and told Stefania what was planned. Then she headed for the gift department to pick up the Christmas-wrapped set and put it in her car.

Excited over her mission, she drove home to Limena and shared all that had happened with her mother. They talked until late and she slept poorly, waiting for morning to come.

CHAPTER TWO

THE DRIVE ON Tuesday morning took an hour and a half. Gabi was familiar with part of the route leading to Venice, but she'd never had a reason to take the turnoff going north to reach Maniago. The picturesque town filled a valley surrounded by the Italian pre-Alps.

Her car's sat-nav helped her drive to a lovely pale pink villa located in the foothills. Gabi found the property enchanting as she made her way along the tree-lined path to the front door carrying Dino's gift.

She rang the bell. Now that she was about to meet Dino, she was feeling nervous for fear she might say the wrong thing. At least his grandmother would be with him. Gabi would follow the older woman's lead.

Soon the door opened. A sober-faced woman in a maid's uniform appeared. She eyed the gift. "*Buongiorno!* You must be Signora Parisi from Padova. Signora Berettini is waiting for you. Come in."

Gabi followed her through a luxurious entrance hall to a set of opened French doors on the left. Her gaze traveled to the elegantly dressed older woman who was probably the same age as Gabi's mother. She detected traces of silver in the woman's black hair. The boy's grandmother was tall and very attractive, but there was such sadness in her eyes.

She asked the maid to take the package and put it on the damask love seat, then turned to Gabi. "Thank you for being on time."

"I enjoy getting up early. It was a beautiful drive and I'm anxious to meet Dino. Is he here?"

"No. He and his father live in a villa on an estate about two minutes away. Luca has already driven him to school. Come and sit down."

The news disappointed Gabi, who didn't understand why his grandmother had asked her to come if he was at school. And why not at Dino's home?

"Thank you." She found an upholstered chair opposite her and took her place.

"Allow me to explain. His father doesn't

know about the letter. If he'd heard about it, he might have discouraged me from sending it in order not to get Dino's hopes up. What if there'd been no response? He adores that child and doesn't want anything to hurt him. That's why I preferred that you and I meet here first."

Gabi nodded. "I can understand that. Edda gave me some background about the avalanche where Dino lost his mother, but she didn't know specifics or why he needs an operation. I honestly don't know how you survive a tragedy like that."

"I'm not sure we're doing it very well," the older woman said in a sad, quiet voice. "But I don't want to dwell on it. What's important is that you've come. It will make him so happy."

"I'm glad Edda sent me."

She wiped her eyes. "I could never deny my grandson anything. He and my son are both in a fragile emotional state at the moment. As the time gets closer to the operation, I'm afraid Luca has grown as anxious as Dino. You see, when my grandson was brought in to the hospital after the avalanche, the scans revealed a benign brain tumor."

"Oh, no."

"The doctor says it's the reason for the headaches. But removing it could cause other complications, increasing our anxiety."

"Of course." Gabi clasped her hands together. "How soon does he have to have it?"

"December twenty-first. That's three weeks from now. The neurosurgeon will fly in to Padova and perform it at San Pietro Hospital."

"No wonder your son is so worried. How frightening for all of you."

"Exactly. But we can't afford to think about anything negative now. The family has videos of Dino with his mother at various ages, and he watches them whenever he misses her too much. I hope that your quick response to Dino's letter and the fact that you came in person will cheer him up even if it can't solve the problem. He's struggling so terribly over the loss of his mother you can't imagine."

Gabi's heart went out to her, to all of them. "The poor thing. Everyone at the foundation is praying for him. Edda sent a gift for him. It's a building blocks game he can put on a table."

Tears kept welling in her blue eyes. "What I'd give if that present and your kindness to come in person will help him face the operation! My son is absolutely desperate." The older woman clasped her hands under her chin.

"Since I want it to be a surprise, this is what I'd like to do. If you'd be willing, I'd like you to follow me to my son's villa."

"Of course." Gabi had made her first phone call there apparently.

"When we get there, I'll go pick him up at school and tell him I have a surprise waiting for him at home. The cook will have our lunch prepared. He'll be delighted to get out early since his father doesn't normally bring him home until one. But not today! I'll leave a message at his office that I wanted to pick him up. That way my son can stay at work longer."

That made sense to Gabi, who was eager to meet Dino.

"When he comes running in the house, he'll see you and the gift. We'll go from there." She stood up and called to her maid.

"He sounded so sweet in his letter, I'm looking forward to meeting him, Signora Berettini."

"He's a combination of imp and angel. I'll get my car and ask Carla to take the present back to yours."

"Thank you."

In a few minutes she found herself following the black Mercedes sedan through the hills.

When she rounded the next corner, she let out a quiet gasp at the sight of a sprawling two-story yellow villa set in the mountain greenery like it had grown there.

From the style, she imagined it had been built in the eighteenth century. Gabi had toured through many splendid villas from the past opened to the public. But she'd never seen anything more gorgeous than this one owned by the wealthy Berettini CEO. How sad his money couldn't fix what was wrong with Dino.

She drove through the gates and went all the way to the circular drive in front, where she parked the car behind Giustina's. After retrieving the gift, she joined her at the entrance, where another woman answered the door who was all smiles.

"Ines? Please meet Gabi Parisi from the Start with a Wish foundation. Gabi? This is the nanny who has looked after our precious Dino with unswerving devotion."

"I'm very happy to meet you, Ines."

"It's a privilege to meet someone from the program we see on TV. He loves it and watches it every time it's on. He won't believe you're here."

"I hope it will bring him some comfort."

"We're counting on it, aren't we, Ines? Will you take this gift into the family room?"

"Si, signora."

They followed her through the magnificent interior to the rear of the villa. It overlooked the breathtaking town with snow-covered summits beyond it in the far distance. Ines placed the present on the big table.

The first thing Gabi saw was the framed photograph of a young woman that hung above the fireplace. With her long dark hair, what a beauty she was! "Is this Dino's mother?"

"Yes. That's Catarina."

Gabi looked around at the warm, friendly room. It was made for a child's pleasure with books and games, comfortable furniture, a TV and several wonderful photographs of animals living in the wilds of Africa.

She turned to Giustina. "A room like this must be heaven for a little boy."

"Dino's mother decorated it. Naturally it's his favorite spot in the villa."

"It would be mine."

"Gabi? I'll leave now to get Dino and won't be long. His school is nearby. I'll ask the maid to bring you tea or coffee. Do you have a preference?"

"Tea would be lovely."

When she left, Gabi walked over to the floor-to-ceiling bookcase to look at them all. There were so many darling storybooks he'd probably been read over and over again.

Ines brought the tea. Now would be a good time to ask a few questions. "Tell me about what Dino is like."

"He's very bright and loves to play with friends. When he doesn't have a headache, you would never know he has a problem. But he still suffers from nightmares to do with the avalanche. It came upon them so fast. When he hears a really loud noise like thunder, he freezes and runs to hide under his bed."

"I can imagine. How horrible for him."

"His father is hoping that once the operation is over, he won't be so anxious about everything."

"The poor dear. What are some of the things he likes?"

"Swimming and comic books. His father won't let him look at *Diabolik* for fear it will give him nightmares, but he's allowed to read *Lupo Alberto*."

"I too loved the comics when I was young." While she was deep in thought, she heard the sound of footsteps running down the hall toward the family room.

Suddenly the boy raced inside but came to a halt when he saw Gabi.

She jumped to her feet, taking in the sight of Dino Berettini in the blue smock all Italian children his age wore to school. He appeared on the taller side of seven with forget-me-not-blue eyes and black shiny hair like his mother's in the photograph. The handsome child didn't look like anything could be wrong with him.

"Hello, Dino."

"Hi! Who are you?"

His grandmother came in the room. "Dino? You should wait to be introduced."

"Sorry, Nonna," he murmured.

"I'd like you to meet Signora Gabi Parisi. She's come all the way from Padova to meet you."

"How do you do, *signora*?" What an adorable boy. "Why have you come to see me?"

Gabi took a deep breath. "Because you sent a letter to the Start with a Wish foundation, right?"

His eyes widened. "You got it already?"

"Yes. That's where I work. Yesterday the mail came and I opened it."

"You did?" He sounded utterly incredulous, then turned to his grandmother. "You said you mailed it, but—"

"You didn't believe me?" The older woman sounded surprised.

"Yes, but… I was afraid it wouldn't get there."

Gabi took a step closer. "Well, it did, and it was my lucky day because my boss said I could come to visit you and bring you a present." During their conversation Gabi had seen his eyes darting to the package on the table.

"You have a boss?"

"Yes. Her name is Edda."

"My *papà* is a boss, too."

She nodded. "He's such an important boss, everyone knows him, even Edda. She was the one who wanted me to bring his son a special surprise in person. Would you like to open it?"

"Yes, but it's wrapped for Christmas."

"That's true, but she said you could open it now if you want. I know if I were in your shoes, I'd run right over to the table and rip off the wrapping paper to see what she sent you."

A smile broke out on his face. No longer hesitating, he rushed toward the table. Gabi's eyes met Giustina's. They both walked over to watch the untidy unveiling.

"A building blocks set!" His happy exclamation told her a lot.

"It's a winter wonderland scene. I bet you can make it look like the one here in Maniago at Christmastime."

Those brilliant blue eyes darted to her. "Can you stay and help me put it together?"

"There's nothing I'd rather do, if it's all right with your grandmother."

"Is it, Nonna?"

"Of course. I'll have lunch served in here while you play."

"Can I call you Gabi?"

"Of course."

"Evviva!"

For the next two hours Gabi had the time of her life helping him put the project together while they ate. They talked about dinosaurs and his favorite emojis. Soon they got on the subject of another comic book character called Tex, from American television; the indomitable hero. Dino was so smart and a perfect delight. You'd never know anything was wrong with him.

Unfortunately, she'd overstayed her welcome

and the time had come when she needed to leave for Padova. Edda would want a report in person before the day was out. "Guess what, Dino? I've had such a terrific time, but now I'm due back at the office."

"No—" he cried out and jumped to his feet. The abrupt change in his demeanor took her by surprise.

"I'm sorry."

Tears filled his eyes. "But I want you to stay."

"I would love to if I could."

"Will you come tomorrow?"

"She has to get back to work," Giustina spoke up. "Now thank her and say goodbye."

"But I don't want her to go." He was relentless. It was an indication of how difficult life could be for him at times. Her heart ached for him and his whole family. His grandmother looked absolutely crushed.

As Gabi turned to leave, he dashed past her and out of the family room.

The older woman seemed frantic. "I'm sorry. I've never seen him act quite like this before."

"He's going through a very difficult time in his life."

"I shouldn't have mailed his letter."

"Don't say that. He loves and trusts you. Now he knows our foundation received it. He believed in something and it happened. That has to have increased the faith he needs to face his operation."

Giustina followed her to the door. "About his letter… There's something I have to tell you before you go. As I told you, his father doesn't know about it. When he finds out, I don't want him to know everything Dino said. It would kill my son if he thought Dino saw him so unhappy all the time."

"I hear what you're saying and will let Edda know."

"Thank you, Gabi."

"Thank you for the delicious lunch. I'm happy to have met you."

Gabi hurried out of the villa to her car. As she started the engine, she looked up and saw Dino standing at an upstairs window staring down at her. *That precious boy.* There was so much sadness in that house, she could hardly bear it as she drove away.

Between the grandmother's pain and the worry in Ines's expression, Gabi couldn't see any happiness. She wished something else could be done, but she didn't know what.

* * *

At four o'clock, Luca ended the staff meeting and headed for home. His mother's earlier message that she'd be picking up Dino had allowed him to get a lot of work done today.

For the last two years Luca had trimmed his work schedule in order to put his traumatized boy first. Because he was no longer in kindergarten, their normal routine had changed.

Monday through Saturday they ate breakfast together first before he drove Dino to primary school at eight o'clock. Then Luca would leave his office in time to pick him up at one o'clock and they'd go home for lunch. After that, Luca would go back to work until five and Dino's nanny, Ines, would take over.

But today had been an exception from start to finish. Now he could enjoy the rest of the time with his son. Maybe they'd go to another hockey match. He liked watching it with Luca.

He got back in his car and drove to Tauriano. He was furious that his father, who'd always been cold and unyielding, seemed especially devoid of human feelings when it came to Dino. He'd always resented Luca's marriage to Catarina, and had passed on a feeling of dislike toward his grandson.

Thank heaven for Luca's mother and Catarina's aunt and uncle Maria and Tomaso, who'd raised her from a young age. They were like another set of grandparents to Dino, and he adored them.

For the next three weeks he needed to fill each day with activities for both of them in order to face the ordeal coming up. Once the tumor had been removed, who knew what other problems might ensue. But right now he needed to shelve that worry and handle the present.

He pulled up to the villa and hurried inside. Since his son was usually in the family room, he headed there first. "Dino? Papà is home!"

There was no answering cry, and nothing from Ines. Luca paused long enough to see a giant set of building blocks on the table. The box it came in showed a winter wonderland scene. A certain amount of work had been done on it already. He was impressed.

Apparently this was a surprise from Luca's mother and that was why she'd gone to pick up Dino today. Maybe he'd gone home with his grandmother for dinner.

Curious, he took the stairs two at a time to the next floor, passing Dino's bedroom on the way to his own suite for a shower. That's when he heard sobbing and opened the door to see Ines sitting on the side of the bed trying to comfort his son. Luca felt like he'd been kicked in the gut.

Ines got to her feet and hurried over to him. Sorrow was written all over her face. "He's had an upset today," she whispered, "but it's not because of a nightmare or a headache. He had a visit from a woman representing the Start with a Wish foundation. She brought him a gift, but when she had to leave, it upset Dino. I'm glad you're home. He'll be much better after talking to you." On that note, she left the bedroom.

Luca walked over to the side of the bed. Dino lay on top of the covers on his stomach, hugging a pillow. He was dressed in a T-shirt and jeans. Luca sat down and began to rub his back.

"Polpetto mio." The meatball endearment he'd used with him forever usually brought a laugh, but not this time. "Want to tell Papà what's wrong?"

He whirled around and sat up. His face was a study in misery. Luca hadn't seen a look like that in a long time. "My *nonna* is mad at me. Did she call you?"

His mother didn't have a mean bone in her body, but clearly something had disturbed Dino to the point of tears. "No. I just got home from work."

"She didn't say anything?"

Luca put up both hands. "I swear it."

"Well, she's going to." He slid off the bed. "And then you're going to be really mad at me."

Since when? What the devil had gone on here? "Why would I be mad?"

"Because… I was rude to Gabi."

Gabi? "Who's that?" he asked, though Ines had already informed him.

"She brought me a present from that *Start with a Wish* program on TV." Luca had heard of it, of course. Who hadn't? How had they known about Dino?

"We were having so much fun putting it together, and then she had to leave and I didn't want her to go. I got so mad I ran out of the room. After I went upstairs, I watched her drive away. And now I know she'll never come back."

He ran to Luca and wrapped his arms around him. "I'll never see her again."

Luca didn't have a clue what was going on,

but with those words, he knew this had something to do with the loss of Dino's mother. Luca needed to stop the bleeding before there was a full-blown emotional hemorrhage.

Gabi arrived at work Wednesday morning, anxious to talk to Edda when she came in. She hadn't been in her office when Gabi returned yesterday. Today she needed to pass on Giustina's concerns about certain contents of the letter and tell her what had happened at the Berettini villa. Dino hadn't wanted her to leave, and heaven help her, she hadn't wanted to leave either.

His quick mind, his laughter, the funny things he said—everything about him tugged at her heart. She'd meant it when she'd told him she'd love a son just like him. It was true. What wasn't there to like? The fact that he was facing a serious operation only made her feelings more tender toward him.

An hour later, in the middle of opening more letters, Stefania told Gabi that Edda wanted to see her in her office. Gabi hadn't realized her boss had already come in.

She excused herself and walked down the hall. Edda welcomed her in and told her to sit down. "I'm happy to inform you that your visit yesterday made a deep impression on Dino Berettini. So much so in fact that he's downstairs in the reception area with his father, who took time off from his work to drive them here. They've come specifically to see you."

What? His father had brought him? Gabi couldn't credit any of it.

"There's more, Gabi. They've asked if you could spend the day with them while they're here in Padova. I told them it would have to be your decision. Of course you have my permission. How do you feel about that?"

How did she feel? "Do you think I should?"

Edda scrutinized her. "Is there a reason you wouldn't want to see him again?"

"No, but I haven't met his father."

"Ah. The idea makes you uncomfortable."

"Not at all, but I'm just surprised he's here. Did you show him Dino's letter?"

"The subject didn't come up. It appears he wants his son to apologize to you in person for the way he behaved toward you before you left their home. He's concerned that Dino ran out on you and didn't say goodbye or even thank you."

She shook her head. "That wasn't important. He was like all children who don't want something fun to end."

"Well, he's here now and waiting to see you. I've informed Stefania."

"Thank you." Gabi stood up. "I'll go down."

"Keep me informed."

"Of course."

Fortunately, Gabi had worn her navy suit with a lighter blue collared blouse to work and felt presentable. She stopped in the conference room for her purse and waved to Luisa, who knew about her visit to Dino. Once outside in the hall, she brushed her hair and put on a fresh coat of pink frost lipstick before she made her way downstairs to the reception room.

People doing business or needing information came to the foundation throughout the day. Gabi looked around at the half-dozen visitors until she saw Dino, who slid off the chair but didn't run to her.

Seated next to him had to be his father, who got to his feet. He was tall and fit, with black hair and blue eyes that matched his son's. The thirtyish male who'd once won an Olympic gold medal for Italy's ski team was beyond gorgeous despite the telltale lines of grief.

She took a quick breath and walked the short

distance to them. "*Benvenuto*, Dino! What a wonderful surprise! Here I thought you were at school this morning."

He looked so solemn. "I asked Papà to drive me here. I'm sorry about yesterday."

Gabi smiled. "I'm not. I had such a great time and didn't want to go back to work. I felt just like you did."

A half smile broke out on his face. "So… you're not mad at me?"

"What do you think?"

A huge smile broke out on his face. Over his dark head her eyes fused with his father's.

"Dino?" the man asked in a deep voice that penetrated her body. "Aren't you going to introduce us?"

His son looked at both of them. "Gabi? This is my *papà*."

CHAPTER THREE

GABI CHUCKLED. "SINCE you two look like each other, I figured he has to be your father. I'm delighted to meet you, Signor Berettini."

The CEO of the Berettini empire had dressed in a charcoal-colored suit with a gray pullover and probably had to shave twice a day. No man's looks or masculine aura had ever given her such a visceral reaction.

Amusement lurked in his eyes fringed with sooty black lashes. He took her breath. "After hearing about Gabi this and Gabi that, I've been the one anxious to meet you," he said, shaking her hand.

She felt the contact zap through her like a bolt of lightning. His blue gaze traveled over her as if he were trying to piece everything together using his son's assessment of her. In truth she'd been doing the same thing to him and hoped to heaven it didn't show.

She looked down at Dino. "Edda told me you wanted to spend the day with me. Guess what? She gave me permission to leave."

"*Evviva!* Do you know where we should go?"

"Since I've lived here all my life, I have a lot of ideas. One of my favorite places is the insect museum in Brusegana."

"Insect—" His reaction was comical.

"That's right. When I was in school, we took a field trip there. I thought it would be stupid until we arrived on the bus. Was I ever wrong! It's a few kilometers from the center of the city."

"Does it have real insects in it?"

"Thousands! Of course, most of them are dead, thank goodness." His father laughed. "It's an amazing museum, Dino. Maybe we could eat lunch at DaPretta's first. It's only a few blocks away. They do fast food and make the most delicious bacon and potato *panzerottos*.

"Afterward we'll drive to Brusegana and spend part of the day there. If you want, we can watch a movie about insects while we're at the museum and buy something in the book shop to add to your collection of books in your family room. I never saw so many. You'll love visiting there!"

His face lit up with excitement. "Papà? Have you been there?"

He shook his dark head. "It'll be a new experience for me, too." His gaze focused on her again, and she felt an instant awareness of him that went deep beneath the surface. "Are you ready to leave?" She nodded. "Then let's go."

Gabi followed them out to the parking area, where he headed for a fabulous dark red Lancia luxury passenger car. While Dino climbed in the backseat and strapped himself in, his father helped Gabi in the front passenger seat. She felt his gaze on her legs as she swung them inside.

His interest was that of any normal male, but she hadn't been with a man in two years. If she was going to be this affected by his every look and touch, maybe she'd made a mistake in not accepting dates from guys since her divorce. But Luca Berettini wasn't just any man.

She'd heard of the expression *coup de foudre*, love at first sight. Gabi had never believed in such a thing, but if it existed she feared it had happened to her.

When they stopped to eat and find a table,

she'd noticed every female in sight, young or old, staring at Dino's striking father and eyeing her with envy for being in his company. She needed to get herself in hand and concentrate on his son. Before long they were served and Dino seemed to like his food.

In a few minutes one of the male servers who was probably Gabi's age left the counter to walk over to them. He stood by Luca. "Excuse me for interrupting, but I know you're Luca Berettini. I saw you win the gold medal in the downhill when I was sixteen. I can't believe you just walked in here. Would you let me take a picture with my phone? My friends won't believe it."

Gabi saw a clouded expression enter Luca's eyes. "I'd rather you didn't."

The guy nodded. "Excuse me, then. But I have to tell you that seeing you has made my day."

When the man walked off, Gabi looked at Luca through shuttered eyes. "I imagine that must happen to you often."

"More than I'd like. If I were alone, it would be different, but not when I'm with my son."

"I would feel the same way," she said in a quiet voice. Every mention of skiing had to be a reminder of Dino's suffering and what his life had once been like before the avalanche. "Luckily he's enjoying his food and didn't seem to pick up on anything."

He darted a glance at Dino. "These *panzerottos* are a definite hit and have provided the needed distraction."

"I've loved them forever. What are your favorite dishes?" Gabi found herself wanting to know everything about him.

His eyes played over her with a definite gleam. "Pizza *patate*."

"Potatoes on pizza. I've never tried it."

"It's the specialty of a place near my work."

She smiled at him. "You mean you don't have your secretary bring in fabulous meals for you every day?"

"Afraid not. I can hardly wait to get out of there and go home to eat. But sometimes I have to stay longer, and a pizza *patate* helps get me through the rest of the long cruel hours."

"I see." Gabi drank the last of her coffee. "Are you telling me you don't like being the CEO of one of the most famous companies in Italy?"

"Would it shock you if I told you it's the last place I want to be?"

Gabi averted her eyes. "Actually it wouldn't, not when you've had something so serious on your mind for the last two years."

He shook his dark head. "That's not the only reason. Before I was forced to take over for my father, I'd been building my own skis and boots manufacturing business. I still run it on the side and have little interest in my family's company. I'm afraid I never will. One day soon when my father is able to take over again, I'll walk away and not look back."

That sounded final. Gabi wiped her mouth with a napkin. She couldn't help but wonder about the history behind it and how his father felt about that, but it was none of her business.

Luca put some bills on the table. "That was delicious."

"I want to come here again," Dino replied.

"Maybe we will. Shall we drive to Brusegana now?"

Dino got up from the table. Luca helped Gabi and they left for his car. It had been a long time since she'd been anywhere with a man, and never with one as appealing as Dino's striking father.

When she'd come to work this morning, she couldn't have imagined his driving to the foundation with his son in order to thank her and give Dino a chance to apologize, let alone spend the day with her. The whole situation had caught her completely off guard.

After a short drive, they pulled in the parking lot of the museum. Luca had a devastating smile. Her pulse raced when he used it on her. "This ought to be interesting."

"I hope so," she said in a slightly breathless voice.

From the moment they walked inside the doors, the three of them were mesmerized by the hundreds of insect displays. For the next hour Dino ran from one to another, marveling over the varieties and colors.

"Gabi—look at this big black one with the orange stripes! Ew. I'd hate to meet that in the forest."

"It's probably pretty harmless."

"How about the sculpture of this giant cicada standing upright?" his father called out. They hurried over to look at it. "He could be a soldier."

The large statues of insects were something new since the last time she'd been here. "I'm thankful they don't grow that huge in real life."

"Except in the movies," Luca murmured.

She chuckled. “I’m afraid I paid a lot of money to watch them in my youth.”

“So has the whole world.” Their eyes met in mutual amusement.

“You mean you liked them, too?”

The corner of his compelling mouth curved upward. “They were the best films to take a girl to.”

His surprising sense of humor got to her. What girl wouldn’t have wanted to go anywhere with him, even a scary show? Every time she looked at him now, her body quivered in reaction.

Dino hurried along to inspect the butterflies. There were hundreds of them.

“I like the black one with the green spokes from Africa. It’s my favorite.”

After Gabi had taken a picture with her phone, his father said, “Let’s go in the theater now. They’ll be starting a movie in a few minutes.”

Somehow she ended up sitting next to Luca at the very back of the auditorium with his son on his other side. Judging by the oohs and aahs coming from the audience, the film engrossed everyone watching, but no one more so than Dino.

"First the food was a huge hit, now the museum," Luca whispered. She felt his warm breath against her cheek. More delicious sensations traveled through her body.

Though she agreed with his assessment, right now she couldn't concentrate on anything except being next to this exciting man. "I thought he'd like it."

"You've made his day. Are you sure you weren't a schoolteacher instead of an employee working at a boring bank job in another life?"

Gabi laughed gently. "I'm going to have to be careful around Dino. He doesn't miss a trick."

"I figure I've heard about your whole life story already. At least the parts you chose to share with him. I guess you know you've made a big impression on him."

She smiled. "He's a very sweet boy. You're so lucky to have him."

"He's my life." The tone in his voice spoke volumes about the love he had for his son.

"Of course he is." But before she could say more, the lights went on because the show was over and Dino expressed a desire to visit the bookstore.

He wanted the big two-feet-by-two-feet colored picture book on insects. Who wouldn't? But Luca walked him around to look at other books just to make certain it was the best one so he wouldn't change his mind. Gabi admired his patience and thoughtful concern.

After they went out to the car, he climbed in back and started poring through the book that would give him hours of pleasure.

She glanced at his father. "See that *gelateria* on the corner? Let's stop and get one, shall we? I'd like to pay for it."

"You're reading my mind, but it will be my treat. For you to have come up with an outing like this means more to me than you know." Once again his voice penetrated to her insides. So did his words that touched her on a deeper level. He parked outside the shop. "Do you have a preference?"

"Any fruit gelato with *panna*." She loved whipping cream.

"I like *fondente* with *panna*, Papà."

Gabi grinned and looked over her shoulder at him. "You like chocolate, eh?"

"Sì." He was still concentrating on the pictures.

She eyed his father, who smiled at her before he said, "I'll be right back."

"I wish we didn't have to go home," Dino admitted after Luca left the car. "I wish—" he began, then stopped.

"You wish what, *piccolo*?"

"That you could be with me when I have my operation."

With those heartfelt words, Gabi had trouble not falling apart. "It's funny about wishes. Sometimes they come true. When I was young, I had a group of friends and we wished on a star for a friend who was very sick. And guess what? She got well. You never know."

"How do you do that?"

"At night you look up in the sky, find a star and make a wish."

"I'm going to do that tonight."

Just then Luca returned and handed her a peach concoction.

Their fingers touched, igniting her senses. Could he tell how the contact affected her? What was wrong with her? "Thank you."

"Prego."

It seemed he was a chocolate lover like his son. Soon they were all enjoying their treat. She eyed his father. "The *panna* on yours looks delicious."

"Papà loves *zabaglione*."

Gabi didn't realize Dino had been listening, and it took her by surprise.

His father darted her a lighthearted glance. "Marsala wine–flavored *panna* is a weakness of mine. You'll have to try it another time."

Maybe when she went out for lunch with Luisa. But she couldn't imagine there'd be another time with Luca Berettini or his son. She pondered that thought all the way back to the parking lot behind the foundation building.

Today's outing had proved that it wouldn't be wise to get any more involved with Dino's father. She'd enjoyed being with him too much. After Santos, she was afraid to get too close to another man again and be hurt. Luca was already an unforgettable man, bigger than life. Something told her that if she were to fall in love with a man like him, she'd never get over it. The possibility of that happening shook her.

Again something had to be wrong with her to even be thinking this way when the Berettini family was facing a huge ordeal in a few weeks. Luca's fear for his son was all that mattered to him.

Gabi had done her part and knew for a fact Luca would never have come to Padova if it hadn't been for her visit on behalf of the foundation. How foolish of her to believe Luca could be romantically interested in her that way. The sooner she got out of the car, the better.

Edda had asked Gabi to follow through on the foundation's commitment to Dino. She'd done everything possible she could. Now she needed to walk away before the attraction to his father and his boy became so great, she couldn't.

After he turned off the engine, she undid her seat belt and looked around at Dino, who had a hold on her emotions. "I'm so glad you came to my work today. I had the best time with you."

"Me, too," he said, but he didn't look up and continued to turn the pages of the book.

"You're the smartest boy I know, and I bet you'll finish your building blocks game by the end of the week."

No response.

"I'll keep you in my prayers. I want you to know you'll always have a friend at the Start with a Wish foundation. Now I have to go in."

She grabbed her purse. In that fleeting moment her gaze met his father's. For the first time all day they were filled with undeniable pain, all of it because of his son. She knew her pain for Dino was reflected in hers, too.

Today had been a lovely moment out of time, but it was over. She opened the door and hurried to the building entrance, but she'd left her heart behind with that child and…heaven forbid, Luca Berettini.

The day had been heavenly for Dino, but unsettling for Luca, who'd been far too aware of Gabi while they'd walked around the museum…connecting. With Catarina's death he'd buried his heart, or so he'd thought. Yet everything about Gabi had brought out feelings he didn't want to experience again. To care for a woman after all this time, to fall in love and then lose her would be too terrible to contemplate. Luca couldn't deal with that.

But as he'd watched Gabi disappear into the building after they'd dropped her off, he'd felt a strange sense of loss that had nothing to do with his son's pain. Luca had been out to dinner with several women since his wife's death, trying to get back to some kind of normal existence. But the nightmare that had taken Catarina's life had left him empty.

Until today…

While he tried to put Gabi out of his mind, the journey back to his villa in Maniago turned out to be the drive from hell. Pure silence accompanied him all the way home. Dino had kept his promise to his father not to cry or protest when they had to say goodbye to her. He'd been a model of obedience. No pleading. No tantrums. That had been the bargain they'd made before they'd ever left the villa.

She lived in another city and had an important job to do. She'd brought his son a gift from the foundation and had shown him unparalleled kindness in answer to his letter, but that was all Dino could expect. That's what he'd told him.

Now his son wasn't talking to him, causing Luca to relive the events of the day in his mind. To his astonishment, he'd found himself enjoying the outing with the beautiful blonde Signora Parisi more than he would have imagined. Her engaging personality had a seductive power that had ensnared his son from the moment he'd first met her. Luca had seen him reach for Gabi's hand several times throughout the day.

But it was in the movie at the museum he'd felt a pull on his emotions that had shocked him. It had been a long time since he'd shared one of those moments that had made him wish he'd known a woman like Gabi in his teens. She had a unique sense of fun, yet showed amazing compassion for his son's fears.

Edda Romano knew what she was doing when she'd hired Gabi to work for her. Gabi had a vivacious quality. When she walked in a room, a light went on, something he hadn't thought could possibly be ignited inside his soul again. Now it seemed Luca himself hadn't escaped the special magic that was as natural to her as breathing.

When they arrived at the villa, Dino carried his book into the family room and put it on the table, ignoring Luca. Ines came in to announce dinner, but his son wanted to show her the book first.

"What amazing pictures! Where did you get it?"

With that question, all the information you could ever want came pouring out of Dino. "Gabi took us to the insect museum in Padova."

"I didn't know there was one."

"Gabi went to it when she was in school. We even saw insects and blue butterflies from Africa!" It had been another connection to Catarina, who'd promised that one day the three of them would go on safari. Dino talked all the way through their meal. Then it was time for his bath and bed.

Tonight Luca took over the duties. But after Dino had said his prayers, he darted over to the window and looked out at the night sky.

"What are you doing, *figlio*?"

"Nothing."

"Then come get in bed."

Dino ran back and climbed under the covers. He looked up at Luca. "Thanks for taking me to see Gabi. I had the best time of my whole life."

More than everything else in his whole life?

Luca swallowed hard. "I enjoyed it, too."

"I wish she lived in Maniago so I could see her every day," he said with tears in his voice. "When I'm with her, I have so much fun and… I'm not as afraid to have the operation. But I know she can't come every day." He half moaned the words.

Oh, Dino. Luca's heart lurched. His son's attachment for Gabi went beyond the superficial. Dino was crazy about her.

"*Buona notte*, Papà." The last was smothered as Dino turned away and buried his face in the pillow.

After turning off the light, Luca disappeared down the hall to his own suite of rooms, aware of a new burden weighing him down. Dino's mother wouldn't be coming back, but Gabi Parisi was alive and living in a city not that far away. No one was more aware of that than Luca, who would like nothing more than to see her again tomorrow.

The woman was beautiful, feminine. During the film in the darkened room, he'd found himself wanting to taste her mouth. They'd sat close enough that it would have been so easy for him to move close enough to kiss her. It had been over two years since Luca had made love to his wife. Today it stunned him that his feelings for Gabi were so strong.

Luca had sensed she was aware of him, too. There were certain signs he'd noticed when their bodies or fingers had brushed against each other by accident, or when she'd thanked him, sounding a little breathless.

There was no doubt she'd made an impact on Dino that wasn't going to go away. Judging from the way she reacted to his son, Gabi had showed him genuine interest and attention. So much so that by the weekend, Dino had become more taciturn than Luca had ever seen him.

He showed no excitement at the hockey match and had stopped working on the project left on the table. The impending operation had to be responsible for part of that behavior, but not all of it. His son wanted to see Gabi again. So did Luca, who was pained by the effort Dino made not to mention her name.

When Luca's mother came over on Sunday for dinner, he didn't want to talk about the outing to Padova. It was too painful for his son. The weekend had been hard on Luca, too.

After he drove his son to school on Monday morning, he had every intention of going to work. But when he reached the highway, something made him turn around and head for Padova. En route he phoned and made an appointment to talk to Edda Romano. As soon as he arrived at the foundation, he was shown upstairs to her office.

"Thank you for seeing me so quickly. I know how busy you are."

She smiled. "Never too busy when this involves your son, who is facing a difficult ordeal. How soon is his operation?"

"December twenty-first."

"I see. What can I do for you?"

"You've already done everything humanly

possible, and I'm deeply grateful. Since you hired Signora Parisi, you have to know she brought sunshine into Dino's life. He had a wonderful time with her last Wednesday and wants to see her again. I realize that wasn't something any of us could have predicted."

"Are you asking my permission for her to spend more time with Dino?"

"After hours, yes. But only if it doesn't break your rules."

"Of course it doesn't! The person you need to ask is Signora Parisi herself."

"But I don't want to make her uncomfortable. Would you be willing to ask her to meet me in the reception room downstairs?"

"Of course."

"Bene, signor. Arrivederci."

Luca left her office with trepidation and went downstairs to wait. Gabi might not want any more contact with him for her own personal reasons. He didn't want her to feel obligated. If she wasn't interested in getting to know him better, that would be the end of it.

CHAPTER FOUR

"GABI?" STEFANIA HAD just returned from Edda's office. "Signor Berettini is downstairs in the reception area waiting for you."

She almost fell off her chair in shock. He was here? Gabi knew she wasn't dreaming. Just the mention of the man's name caused a small gasp to escape her throat. "Do you know what it's about?"

"I have no idea."

"I'll go now. Thanks."

She reached for her purse and hurried downstairs, embarrassingly breathless when he saw her coming and walked toward her. Darn if her heart didn't leap at the sight of him. "Signor Berettini—" Her hand went to her throat. "Has something happened to Dino?"

"Only that he's missing you and wishes he could see you again."

"You mean it?" she cried softly, giving herself away. “I’d love to see him again, too. He’s a wonderful boy!” And so was his father.

“He feels the same way about you. Why don’t we go out for a cappuccino and plan something? I’ve already checked with Edda.”

“I’d like that.”

“If you’re ready.”

She nodded and he walked her out to his car. He was wearing navy trousers and a crew neck matching sweater. With his hard-muscled physique, he looked magnificent in anything.

She really couldn’t believe this was happening. Adrenaline kept her pulse racing. “Where are we going?”

“I thought we’d visit the James Bond Bar at the Abano Grand Hotel for the fun of it.”

Fun. When had she ever had fun like this? “I’ve heard about it but have never been there.”

Gabi felt like she was floating. For the rest of last week, she’d wondered if there was something wrong with her because she’d been reliving the day with Dino and his father to the exclusion of all else.

She’d wanted to do something like it again, but had given up hope such a thing would happen. In fact, there’d been moments when she’d wanted to call Dino’s grandmother and find out how he was doing, but she hadn't dared. Now because of his father's visit to the foundation, Gabi was going to see him again and spend this beautiful morning with Luca.

Her heart pounded crazily while he walked her into the bar, famous for the selection of cocktails created as a tribute to the famous 007. But when the waiter came over to their table, Luca ordered cappuccinos and croissants. "Unless you'd like a martini, shaken but not stirred."

Gabi laughed gently. "Not this early, in fact hardly ever."

"My feelings exactly."

"Not even while you were winning medals at ski races?"

"Especially not then. You have to keep your wits."

She studied his arresting features. "I admire you for that."

He winked at her. "The nondrinking, or the racing?"

"Both, if you want to know."

"Would it surprise you to know that if you hadn't agreed to come with me this morning, I was virtually at my wit's end?"

All of a sudden their conversation had taken

a downturn. She took a bite of croissant. "Why is that?"

"Dino hasn't been the same since our outing. I'm afraid that's my fault. I told him that when we said goodbye to you at the museum, I didn't want there to be any tantrums."

"That's why he was so quiet on the drive home."

"Dino only speaks when spoken to now and has suffered another headache."

"Oh, no!"

"It's all right. He would have had the headache no matter what had happened. But he's so unhappy, I had to see you again. I figured that if you turned me down this morning, I wouldn't be able to cope any longer."

The honesty of this father gave her insight into his torment. Gabi was thrilled, not only because his son missed her so much, which was very touching, but to realize that Luca had driven all this way to be with her in person when a phone call would have sufficed. Her instincts told her Luca wanted her company, and not just for Dino's sake.

"I have an idea. I could get off early from work tomorrow and drive to Maniago. Depending on the traffic I could be there close to six."

She heard his sharp intake of breath. "We'll be waiting for you when you drive up to the house, and we'll go out for a meal. How does that sound to you?"

"I'll love it."

"Do you have a preference?"

"No. I like surprises, just like this one."

"So do I, and you're one of them. *Grazie, signora*," he said with what sounded like heartfelt sincerity. She knew Dino's father was relieved. Since their outing, she'd dreamed about being with him to the point she'd been thinking about him all day long, too. Gabi had even wished on a star in order to see him again.

"My name is Gabi."

She heard his low chuckle. It sent curls of warmth through her. "Don't I know it! When you came to our home last week, Dino never stopped saying it."

"The joys of fatherhood."

"It has its moments."

Gabi envied him, no matter how much pain he was in. "I'll see you tomorrow. In case I haven't said so before now, I'm glad you talked to Edda this morning. She's very understanding of Dino. I can't wait to see him again. Now I'd better get back to work, *signor.*"

"Luca, please."

"Luca it is."

He put some bills on the table, and they left the hotel to reach his car. Christmas decorations were everywhere. For a minute, as she walked with the man who had a stranglehold on her heart, she could dream she was in the middle of the winter season Dino was building. When they reached her office and said goodbye, Gabi was so excited for the next day, she knew she wouldn't close her eyes all night.

After work that evening, she walked over to the worktable in her bedroom and pulled down her fourteen-by-eighteen sketch pad from the shelf. Since the visit to the museum, Gabi had been making a drawing of the black-and-green butterfly Dino had loved from her phone photo, not knowing when there'd be an opportunity to give it to him.

Now she needed to color it with the pastels to make it come to life. She'd already signed it "Gabi," and had written the date they'd gone to the museum beneath it. Tomorrow she'd buy a frame with clear glass on her lunch hour and mount the drawing. When she saw Dino later, this would be her personal gift to him. She couldn't wait to surprise him!

In truth, Gabi couldn't wait to be with Luca again either.

Luca told Ines and their cook, Pia, that he and Dino would be eating out. He'd debated whether to tell his son the news early. In the end he decided it would be much more exciting for him to walk out the front door and discover Gabi parked in the drive.

At ten to six Luca went to the family room and shut off the TV. "Come on, Dino. We're leaving. Grab your jacket."

"Where are we going?"

"Out to dinner."

"I don't want to go anywhere."

"You'll change your mind when you find out who's going with us." He left the room and started down the hall to the foyer.

"But we were with my *nonni* last night. Is it Signorina Gilbert? I heard them talking about her. I don't want you to marry her."

Luca was furious at his father for talking about it in front of Dino, who picked up on everything. "I'd never marry her."

"Promise?"

"I swear it. This is a happy surprise. Now let's go." He opened the front door and headed for his car in the dark. Dino followed him and climbed in the back, fastening his seat belt. Luca got behind the wheel and backed out to the street, where he pulled the car to the side. "Why are we stopping?"

"You'll see."

A minute later he saw headlights in his rearview mirror and waited for Gabi to park behind him. That's when he turned to Dino. "Why don't you get out and see who pulled up? She's come to have dinner with us."

Dino got out of the car. Luca followed.

"Gabi?" Even in the dark he could tell his son's countenance had completely changed. *"Evviva!"*

Luca watched his son hug Gabi around the waist. In that revealing moment she hugged him back. Her feelings for his son were just as strong. He knew he'd done the right thing to bring them together.

"Look, Papà! She's brought me another present."

Another Christmas-wrapped package. "I can see that." There were too many of them. "I'll put it in the car."

Before long they were settled in the Lancia and Luca drove them down to the town. Dino talked his head off answering her questions. When they stopped for pizza and salad, Luca carried her gift inside so Dino could open it.

His son had told him that Gabi had wanted to go to art school. But he had no idea how talented she was until Dino pulled the wrapping away and the butterfly from Africa appeared in all its glory. While an astonished Luca stared at it, Dino went into ecstasy.

"I love it, Gabi. I'm going to hang it over my bed."

"I'm glad you like it, *tesoro*." Gabi had used the endearment so naturally, she sounded like any mother with her child. Luca was so deeply touched, he couldn't say anything for a minute, but it didn't matter. The two of them were engrossed talking about what he'd learned in school earlier in the day.

While Dino left the table long enough to use the restroom, Luca eyed the gorgeous woman who had been on his mind day and night. "Quick, before he comes back, would you be willing to spend the coming weekend with us?

"We have a guest bedroom that will be yours while you're there. I realize you probably have other plans, but I confess that I don't want to try and get through another weekend without you." After being with Gabi at the bar and again tonight, Luca couldn't wait to get to know her better. In fact, he needed to be with her so badly he could taste it.

A stillness surrounded her. He could tell he'd taken her by surprise. Before she could answer him, Dino came running back. "Can we go home and play a game now?"

Luca put some bills on the table. "I'm afraid Gabi has to get back home."

The time had passed too fast.

As they walked out of the pizzeria and left for home, Luca's frustration grew because he was aware she still faced the hour-and-a-half drive back to Padova. It wasn't fair to her to come such a long way for such a short period of time. Worse, she hadn't answered his question.

After pulling behind her car, he kept his headlights on and started to get out of the car to help her. But she'd undone her seat belt and had turned to Dino.

"Guess what? Your *papà* has invited me to come spend this weekend with you."

Dino undid his seat belt and sat forward. "He did?"

Gabi shot Luca a glance before she said, "Yes! I think it would be fun. On Saturday we could go get a Christmas tree and decorate it. I saw some for sale in the town while I was driving through. What do you think?"

"A real tree?"

"How about it, Papà?" she asked Luca. "Maybe after we're through, we can go Christmas shopping and walk around the town eating our heads off."

"Can you stay at our house all night?"

"Yes, she can," Luca spoke up before she could answer Dino. "On Sunday we'll put a new puzzle together and work on your Christmas scene."

"Do we have to wait until Saturday?"

She leaned over the seat and ruffled his hair. "I have to work, but we can talk to each other on the computer. You're supposed to be learning your computer skills for school, right? Tomorrow you can send me an email and tell me what you learned in class. When I get home, I'll write you back. How does that sound?"

"I'll send you a whole bunch of stuff."

"Wonderful! Now I'd better get going."

They walked her to her car. Luca opened the

door for her. “Thank you for driving all this way. Be careful going home.”

Her eyes lifted to his. “I promise I will. We’ve got Saturday to look forward to.”

Indeed they did. She wouldn’t have agreed to come if she didn’t want to. Luca would be counting the hours. The next time they were together, he intended to get her alone. He could hardly think about anything else.

They waved goodbye.

Life would be different this week now that his son knew he’d be seeing Gabi again. The rest of Luca’s workweek would be different, too. He’d manage to get through it now because in the next few days she’d be with them.

Dino carried his framed butterfly inside. After his bath and prayers, he got in his bed. Luca gathered what he needed to hang it above him. Trust his son to put his pillow on the other end so he could look up at her artwork. “She’s *molto bello*, Papà.”

Yes, Gabi was awesome. “Don’t forget to get under your covers.”

“I won’t. Tomorrow will you help me send her an email? I want to surprise her.”

“Si, figlio mio. Dormi bene.”

As he walked out of the bedroom he heard him say, "I wish she lived in Maniago."

Luca smiled. His son would beat a daily trail to Gabi's door no matter how he had to do it.

As for himself, Luca didn't dare say what he wished for, but it was a given he wouldn't be far behind his son. If he could have his heart's desire, he'd hold her in his arms and kiss her senseless. Gabi was in his blood.

Emails flew back and forth for the rest of the week. Dino mentioned his friend Paolo many times. With his father's permission, he'd talked Gabi into coming on Friday evening and staying until Sunday afternoon. That would give them more time to do all the plans he had in mind.

But Gabi suffered an emotional panic attack when she realized how strongly attached she was to Dino. In her love for him and the ordeal he was facing, it had made her vulnerable. Though she refused to believe that anything could go wrong during the operation, a part of her wondered how she would handle it if she had to suffer another loss in her life.

And what about his father? She could hardly

breathe when she was around him now. It frightened her that Luca had become so important to her in such a short amount of time. What if he wasn't interested in her? What in heaven's name was she doing allowing herself to get close to him?

On Friday after work, Gabi's mother walked her out to the car. "What's wrong, honey?"

"The truth is, I'm concerned because Dino is growing more dependent on me, but I can't help it."

"Of course you can't. This goes deep with you. The divorce so early in your marriage didn't give you time to try and have another baby. I certainly understand the appeal of this boy who has opened up his heart to you. He's responding to you like you're his *mamma*."

Gabi nodded. "I know you must be worried, too. I'm wondering what's going to happen after he has the operation, but I don't have an answer."

"I know you love him."

"Anyone would," she murmured.

"I think you're crazy about his father, too."

She hid her face in her hands. Her mother knew her through and through.

"Signor Berettini is a pretty irresistible

force. I know of his reputation and have seen pictures of him in the media."

"There's no one like him and… I'm hugely attracted to him. That's my dilemma. I know he's doing whatever it takes to help his son get through this frightening time. The letter Dino sent wanting a miracle brought the three of us together, but after the operation I have no idea what things will be like. Any interest Luca has in me is connected with Dino. I wish I knew how to distance myself from his father."

"No one knows that. You're going to have to take all this on faith."

"You're right," she whispered.

"Go and enjoy this special time. Remember you're helping Dino and his father prepare for the operation. Be part of the miracle."

She nodded, not wanting to risk more pain in her life, but no human could avoid it. She hugged her mother through the open window. "Love you to pieces. Stay safe. We'll keep in touch throughout the weekend."

On the trip to Maniago, Gabi went over their conversation in her mind. She had witnessed several miracles in her life. By the time she reached the house, she'd made up her mind to take her mother's advice. *Be part of the mir-*

acle. One of the ways Gabi could do it was to be as happy and upbeat as possible to get rid of the sadness pervading the villa.

When she pulled up in front of the entrance, Dino came running out the doors. "Gabi—" he called to her and opened the rear door to reach for her suitcase. "I've been waiting for you!"

She smiled. "Hi, *piccolino*! I came as fast as I could."

While getting out, she noticed Luca's powerful silhouette outlined by the foyer lights. The sight of him caused a fluttery feeling in her chest. He caught up with Dino. Together the three of them went inside.

"Dino? Will you take my suitcase in the family room?"

"Yup." He took off.

Luca's blue eyes played over her. "We're glad you arrived here safely."

"So am I. Thank you."

Everything he said and did excited her. It wasn't something she could prevent. In the letter, Dino had talked about his father never being happy. Gabi would do whatever she could to erase those grief lines.

"Why didn't you let me take your suitcase upstairs?"

"Because I have a couple of presents to give out first."

"For me?" Dino had reappeared.

"What do you think?" Gabi teased. She walked to the family room and opened the suitcase. Inside she reached for two gaily wrapped gifts. "You'll have to open these at your own peril."

He eyed Luca, who stood nearby with his hands on his hips in a totally striking masculine stance. "What does she mean?" Dino was so cute.

His father's lips twitched. "I think she's brought something that will surprise you. Why don't you open the package with the Christmas elves first?"

Dino reached for it and took off the paper. He held up the box with the cellophane top. When he realized what it was, he stared at Gabi in shock. "These are chocolate-covered *insects*!"

"That's right. Worms and crickets. They're nummy. Did you know one cricket gives you more protein and amino acids than a serving of fish or beef?"

Luca's head reared and he let out a deep, rich laugh that resonated in the whole room.

"Have you ever eaten one?" came Dino's earnest question.

"Sure. I'll eat one of your crickets now." He handed Gabi the box. She lifted off the lid and put one in her mouth.

Dino looked horrified. "What does it taste like?"

"Chocolate."

He giggled nervously before looking at his father. "Are you going to eat one, too?"

Luca flashed her a smile before he reached for a worm. He put it in his mouth and munched. "Gabi is right. It tastes like chocolate."

"Did you know that two billion people in the world eat insects as part of their diet? The most common are beetles, wasps, bees and caterpillars."

He frowned. "I don't think I want to try one."

"That's all right. Why don't you open your other gift?"

"Okay." But he wasn't nearly as enthusiastic.

"I brought you a pack of twenty treats in blueberry, grape, orange and strawberry flavors so you can give one to every student in your class."

"Um… *Suckers!*" He pulled one out. "What's that in the center?"

"A cricket."

Once again his father roared with laughter.

"Oh." Dino thought about it and put it back in the box.

"Aren't you going to thank her for the gifts?"

"*Si*, Papà."

Gabi decided to take pity on Dino. She drew one more present out of her suitcase and handed it to him. Luca just shook his head. She grinned. "I think you'll like this better."

After removing the paper, he took off the lid and smelled the contents. "Chocolate *bocci* balls! *Evviva!*" In the next minute he'd eaten two of them before hugging her. "Thanks for everything."

"You're welcome."

"I promise I'll try an insect pretty soon."

"You don't have to eat one if you don't want to, but you can have a lot of fun with your friends at school. You could give one to your teacher and see if she'll eat it in front of the class."

He thought about it. "I bet she won't."

"What about Paolo?"

"I don't think he'll want to eat one."

"You never know," his father said, winking at Gabi. "Shall we go upstairs and show you where you're going to sleep?"

"That would be lovely."

Dino grabbed her hand while Luca carried her suitcase. The stunning guest bedroom in peach colors was an absolute dream. They agreed to meet downstairs in ten minutes to play a game before Dino had to go to bed.

Gabi took advantage of the time to freshen up. From the bedroom window the lights of the town looked like fairyland. Dino had been born into a very special household. But rich or poor, he had a father who doted on him, and there was no greater blessing. She applied more lipstick and ran a brush through her hair before going back down to the family room.

"Come over to the table, Gabi. We're going to play *guardie e lardri*."

She'd loved cops and robbers when she'd been little.

"I haven't played that in years. Is Ines going to play with us?"

Luca shook his head. "She and Pia have the next two days off."

A delicious shiver ran down Gabi's spine. The three of them would be alone.

"We'll guard the treasure and fight Papà."

Gabi made a face. "How sad for him because we're not going to let him get near it!"

Her comment brought a gleam to Luca's eye while Dino laughed. They played for an hour, but in the end his father proved to be an indomitable opponent. She smiled at Dino. "Even if your *papà* beat us this time, we'll do a rematch tomorrow night and win!"

Luca eyed her with a devilish grin. "We'll see about that. Now it's time for bed."

"Not yet," Dino protested.

"Afraid so, but we'll have all day tomorrow to have fun."

"I know. Gabi? Will you come up while I go to bed?"

"Of course."

"Leave all your chocolates down here, son."

"*Si*, Papà."

She followed Dino out of the room and up the stairs to his bedroom. Hers was farther down the hall. The first thing she saw when she walked in was her butterfly hanging over his headboard.

"Papà put your picture right there."

"So I see."

"I look at it every night."

She couldn't believe the thrill it gave her. Dino lived in a room made for a boy with signs of hockey equipment and several large posters of hockey and soccer heroes. "I'll brush my teeth and be right back."

"I'll be waiting." While he was in the bathroom she studied the small framed photos of his family. The consequences of that avalanche had changed their lives forever. Through unimagined circumstances, it was changing hers, too.

Dino came out a minute later wearing Harry Potter pajamas and knelt down at the side of the bed. "I love my *papà* and my *nonna*, and Maria and Tomaso. Please bless Ines and Pia."

Gabi noticed Dino didn't ask for a blessing on his grandfather. Something was wrong there. She'd sensed there was a problem when Luca had told her about taking over for his father at work.

"Please bless me not to be scared of my operation. Please bless Gabi that she'll never leave. Amen."

CHAPTER FIVE

NEVER LEAVE. ONE OF the wishes that lay at the heart of Gabi's turmoil.

"Amen," sounded the vibrant voice of Dino's father, who'd walked over to the other side of the bed to hug him.

Gabi waited until Dino had climbed under the covers, fighting the instinct not to kiss him. "Get a good night's sleep, Dino. We have a big day planned tomorrow. *Buona notte*," she said to both of them. Without looking at Luca, she exited the room.

Once past the door, she hurried to the guest bedroom to get ready for bed. But before getting out a nightgown and toiletries from her suitcase, she was drawn to the huge window to look up at the sky. It had been a glorious day, and an even more magnificent night. The cold made the canopy of stars twinkle, creating a magical scene. While she stood there mesmerized, she heard a knock on the door. "Dino?"

"No. It's Luca. I need to talk to you for a moment."

Her pulse suddenly sped up. "Come in."

Dino's virile father walked in and approached her, still wearing the white pullover and gray trousers from earlier. This close to him, she could smell the soap he'd used in the shower.

Yes, she'd been married to a good-looking man, but it was no use pretending Luca wasn't the most attractive male she'd ever seen or known in her life, physically and otherwise. With the contrast of his black hair and brilliant blue eyes, Luisa would call him the hunkiest man alive, and she'd be right.

For days now Gabi had been telling herself it was Dino she was crazy about. But as she studied his father's hard-boned features and the five o'clock shadow on his chiseled jaw, she couldn't lie to herself any longer. The two men, one young and one in the prime of his life, had pulled her into their gravity field. There was no escape because she knew she was desperately in love.

"Is everything all right?"

"Yes, but I couldn't talk to you the way I wanted around Dino."

"You think he's asleep now?"

"I'm sure of it. He had a big day."

She nodded and looked up at the sky again. "The view from this window is incredible."

"You're right."

"The stars are so bright, you feel like you could reach up and pull one down. It's a Christmas sky. As you're here, how would you like to wish on a star with me for Dino?"

He studied her features. "I've never tried it."

"When I was around twelve, one of my close friends almost died from a burst appendix. Our group decided to get together and wish on a star to make her better. Within twenty-four hours, we heard from her mother that she'd started to get well. It was like a miracle. I want one for Dino."

"Let's do it," he said in a husky voice.

Gabi took a moment to say a silent prayer, the kind she'd uttered years ago with a child's faith.

Star light, star bright. First star I see tonight. Send your light to help Dino not be afraid of his operation.

When she'd finished and looked at Luca, he was still making his wish. What a gorgeous man he was.

When he opened his eyes, the two of them stared at each other for a long moment. Luca rubbed the back of his neck, as if he didn't know what to say next. She knew it was very unlike the charismatic man who ran a business empire. His rare show of vulnerability tugged at her emotions.

"There's no way to tell you how thankful I am that you're here," he began. "Losing his mother changed Dino. I can't get him back, yet he's a different child when you're with us. I know you didn't expect anything like this to happen when you answered his letter with a personal visit and gift. I guess that's what I wanted to say before you went to bed."

Gabi had to silence a moan. When she'd heard him say that he couldn't get his son back, she'd detected his pain. "Surely you know your son worships the ground you walk on, Luca."

He folded his arms across his chest. "I know he loves me, but there are times when I don't seem to be able to reach him."

She took a quick breath. "Maybe it's a case that he feels he can't reach you."

A frown marred his striking features. "What do you mean?"

Gabi couldn't let him go on thinking he'd lost touch with his son even if she'd promised Giustina she wouldn't say anything.

"I wouldn't have missed this experience for anything in the world, Luca. Dino is a dear boy with that childlike faith that makes the world a better place for simply being around him. Now I'm going to tell you something you don't know about the letter he sent to the foundation. I've decided you need to hear everything right now."

He blinked. "I don't understand."

"Then I'll explain. Your mother didn't tell you the whole content of the letter. In fact, she decided she wouldn't tell you until after the operation was over. Maybe not even then because she was afraid it might hurt you too much to know what has been in Dino's heart."

A haunted look crept into his eyes. "Why? Don't keep me in suspense."

"I memorized Dino's letter. He wrote, 'Every night I tell God I'm afraid to have the operation because my *mamma* died and won't be with me. But if it will take away my headaches and make my *papà* happy again, I'll do it. He's never happy and I love him more than anyone in the entire world."

With those words, there was silence followed by a transformation that came over Luca. Tears entered his fabulous blue eyes. She put a hand on his arm.

"Yes, he loved his mother and will miss her forever. But you've always had your son. Don't you see? He's praying for a miracle that will make *you* happy again. That's more important to him than anything else. I don't know of a child who could love his father more than Dino loves you. You needed to know that."

He shook his head. "All this time he's been worried about *my* unhappiness?"

She nodded. "He's your son and has your kind of compassion. That makes you both unique in this world."

A sigh sounded deep in his throat. "You always manage to say the right thing at the right time with a touching sensitivity that speaks to me."

In the next breath he cupped her face in his hands and lowered his mouth to hers. Gabi moaned as their bodies came together and they began kissing each other, one after another until she stopped counting.

Soon she lost track of time and got lost in his arms, never wanting to be anywhere else. The things his mouth was doing to her filled her with the kind of rapture she'd never known or imagined. When he finally lifted his head for air, she didn't want to let him go. But he had more willpower than she did and removed his hands. His breathing had grown shallow.

"The last thing I want to do is walk away from you tonight, but you're a guest in my home and it's time to say good-night. You'll never know what the revelation about that letter has done for me. *Dormi bene, bellissima.*"

The way he'd said *bellissima* melted her bones. Gabi felt new energy radiate from him as he strode to the other wing of the villa on his long, powerful legs. She shut the door and got ready for bed. Once she'd pulled the covers over her, she buried her face in the pillow. This time tears of joy trickled out of the corners of her eyes. Being part of the miracle was a wonderful thing.

Luca got up early Saturday morning a new man, but he didn't know how he'd had the strength of will not to take Gabi to bed last night. Her breathtaking response to his love-making had swept him away.

He stood under the shower reliving those moments in her arms. Before the day was out, he'd get her to himself again because he needed her like he needed the sun on his face.

After pulling on jeans and a sweater, he hurried downstairs to fix breakfast for the three of them. Last night he'd slept better than he'd done since the avalanche. Like an omen, the sun had come out.

He checked the calendar on his watch. Two weeks from today Dino would undergo his operation. *Grazie a Dio* that time would be here before they knew it. Throughout the lead-up, Gabi would be here for his son to cling to.

When Dino walked in the kitchen wearing pants and a pullover, Luca plucked him from the floor and gave him a huge hug.

"*Whoa.* Papà."

Luca chuckled. "Sorry. I was just happy to see you." No sign of a headache or nightmare with Gabi here.

His son smiled at him. "Me, too." He kissed his cheek before Luca put him down. "I thought Gabi would be down, but I guess she's still in bed."

"I'm sure she is, *polpetto mio*. She works long, hard hours every day, and last night she had to drive all this way after work."

"How soon can I go up and get her?"

"Give me time to cook the frittatas first, then you can knock on her door and tell her we're ready to eat. Why don't you set the table?"

Dino got busy. "Do you think she likes apple juice?" He pulled the bottle out of the fridge and put it on the table with three glasses.

"I don't know. Maybe at home she likes beetle juice."

"She wouldn't drink that!" He made a gagging sound.

"What wouldn't I drink?" sounded a familiar female voice. Gabi walked in the kitchen wearing a Christmas-red sweater and black wool pants. Between the feminine mold of her body and her tousled ash-blond hair, Luca could hardly take his eyes off her.

Dino ran over to her and gave her a hug around the waist. "Beetle juice."

"That's one of my favorites, but only on picnics," she teased him. "In the mornings I love apple juice." Her gaze flew to Luca. "I didn't know you were a chef as well as a boss."

His son giggled. "He's not a chef. You're funny, Gabi."

"He looks like one to me."

"Let's hope you approve of my efforts. Breakfast is ready," he announced and put their plates of food on the table.

"Mmm. It smells wonderful." They all sat down. "Does your *papà* cook like this for you every morning?"

"Hardly ever. That's because you're happy today, huh, Papà?"

"You'd better believe it."

Luca trapped her gaze while silent words passed between them. Clearly she'd identified the key to keep Dino on an even keel while they got through the countdown. His son ate with a big appetite. Things couldn't be better. "What do you want to do first today?"

"Can we go get a tree, Papà, and lots of lights?"

"We'll do it. After that we'll have lunch and go to a movie."

"And tonight we'll set it up in the living room! This is going to be the best day of my life!"

He smiled to himself. Whenever the three of them were together, his son said it was the best day of his life. What was even more true was that every day she was with him and Dino, it was the best day of Luca's.

"Since your father made such a delicious breakfast, what do you say we do the dishes? Come on. While you clear the table, I'll put everything in the dishwasher."

Dino jumped up and started to help.

Luca darted her a speaking glance. "I can see I'm superfluous around here, so I'll make sure everything is locked up tight."

Before long they walked out to the car and left for town like any family out for a fun Saturday together. But they needed to bundle up because the temperature had fallen during the night. Before the day was out, Luca predicted snow.

For the moment it felt like they were a real family. Which was a huge problem for Luca, who was having trouble remembering Gabi wasn't his wife or Dino's mother.

Last night after wishing on a star, Gabi had told him everything that had been in his son's letter. The truth of it had helped him see the situation through clear eyes. Being with her last night had also aroused the kind of desire he hadn't felt since before the avalanche. After losing Catarina, he hadn't thought it possible to feel it again.

Gabi had to know he wanted her. There'd been no doubt about it last night. But only time would reveal where both their feelings were leading. She'd brought happiness to his son for the first time in two years, and Dino's needs had to come first right now. It meant Luca had to show some restraint around her. He hadn't mistaken emotions of gratitude for desire, but he needed to take a step back.

In two weeks Dino would have his operation. No one knew how it was all going to turn out. Luca couldn't allow anything to upset the balance of a precarious situation. The only solution for now was to show some discretion with Gabi.

"Look up the street, Papà! There are the Christmas trees Gabi saw."

Luca had seen them among all the holiday decorations and noticed a sign that said the trees could be delivered. Since Dino wanted a big tree, that would solve a problem for taking one home with them. Once they'd picked out the Noble fir they all loved, his son was disappointed they would have to wait until five in the evening for the tree to arrive at the house.

Gabi squeezed his shoulder. "That tree is so big, it would stick out on both ends of your father's car and bump into the ones in front and behind it." Dino's giggle made Luca laugh. "But if you want, we could buy a baby tree instead that would fit right on top. What do you think?"

His son pondered her question. "No. I want the big one. I guess I'll have to wait."

She kissed his cheek. "Hey—we'll be gone most of the day. When we get home, the tree will arrive. Right?"

"Right!"

Crisis averted, all because of Gabi, who was an original and handled his son with all the clever inspiration of a mother. Luca had never planned to replace Catarina. And then this amazing woman had come along…

They walked around buying Christmas presents at the Christmas market with all the wooden huts selling their crafts. There was a life-size nativity scene with real animals Dino loved. After a while they went to a children's Christmas movie and then headed home just as snow started to fall. Dino put his head back and let the flakes melt on his tongue. They all did the same thing during an outing of pure joy.

By the time the tree arrived and the deliverymen had set it up in a corner of the living room, the Berettini villa looked like Christmas had already come.

While they'd been in town, Gabi had never had so much fun and had picked out half a dozen pots of red flowers to decorate the house. With Luca's help, they draped garlands of greenery over the fireplace, the doorways of the main floor, even the magnificent grandfather clock in another corner of the living room.

After he'd strung the lights and put the glittering star at the top of the tree, Luca went out to the kitchen to make them sandwiches and hot chocolate.

Gabi in turn started putting on the ornaments while Dino hung the elves he'd personally picked out with their funny faces. "Where are your old ornaments, *piccolino*? Do you want to get some of them out?"

"We never had a tree before."

"Oh! I didn't realize."

"I'm glad Papà got us one."

"So am I." Gabi knew a lot of families who didn't put up a tree, but she'd always wanted one and her parents had gone along with her wishes. When she'd mentioned getting a tree in front of Dino, Luca hadn't said a word against it.

He eventually came in the room and put on some Christmas music while they ate and wrapped the nutcrackers Dino had picked out to give for his Christmas presents to everyone. After they'd placed the gifts under the tree, they put the crèche together.

Gabi had spent her own money buying them a nativity scene for an early Christmas present. She wanted to help Dino put it together on the coffee table before he went to bed. He seemed delighted over it.

"It's funny to think of Jesus being a baby."

Gabi smiled at Dino's down-bent head as he lay it in the manger. "I agree it's hard to realize he started out his life just like all of us. When I think of my father, I can't imagine him a baby," she murmured as she put a lamb near the crèche.

"Nonna has a picture of Papà when he was a day old. He had a dress on."

How Gabi would love to see it! "My grandmother had a baby picture of my father. He was in a dress, too."

They both laughed.

"Mamma didn't put one on *me*, huh, Papà."

"No. You were wearing a hospital gown in the nursery."

Gabi wanted to see everything, but stopped short of saying as much in case it was too sensitive a subject. Needing to change the direction of conversation, she rose to her feet. "What a mess we've made!" She started cleaning up and took the tray out to the kitchen.

Luca went for the vacuum, and soon the room looked perfect. Gabi stood behind Dino with her arms around his neck while they admired their surroundings. "In one day we've transformed this room into Babbo Natale's workshop. I think we're pretty good elves."

"Me, too. I can't wait for Paolo to come over so I can give him the skinny Red King wooden nutcracker. He'll laugh his head off."

"I'm sure he will." Gabi leaned over and kissed the top of his head. "Do you know I'm anxious to meet him? Maybe he can visit some time and help us finish your building blocks project. You can offer him a treat."

Dino turned around and looked up at her with shining eyes. "Do you think he'll eat one of my chocolate-covered insects?"

"Hmm." She cocked her head. "He's your friend. You know him better than I do."

Luca walked over and picked him up. "Why don't you dare him, and see what happens? While you're thinking about that, it's time to get ready for bed."

"I don't want to go up yet."

"But *we* do. We're exhausted."

Dino jerked his head toward Gabi. "Are you tired?"

"I'm afraid I'm very tired," she lied. Luca's blue eyes thanked her.

"Tutto bene." He'd caved, but he didn't sound happy about it.

Together they headed upstairs and went through Dino's nightly ritual until he'd said his prayers and had climbed under the covers. "How long are you going to stay tomorrow?"

Gabi had known that question was coming. "For as long as I can before I have to drive back. How does that sound?"

"Why do you have to work?"

She eyed Luca, feeling helpless. "Why does your father work?"

"He says it's so we can eat."

"Your *papà* is right. How else could I have bought those nummy insects for you? Just remember that one day you'll have to work so *you* can eat."

After a silence, "Gabi? I love you."

"I love you, too. Now go to sleep. I'll see you in the morning."

"I love you, too, Papà."

She watched Luca lean down and kiss his son before they left the bedroom and went back downstairs to the living room. The scent of the pine tree had already filled the air. Between all the decorations, Gabi felt like they'd walked into a Christmas wonderland. She sat down on the couch while he rearranged a couple of the elves that were too close together.

"Why did you buy a tree when you've never done it before?"

He turned around. "Dino lit up when you suggested it. Before the avalanche, we always spent our Christmas holidays at the chalet in Piancavallo so we could ski. With trees all around in the mountains, we didn't need one.

"As for the last two years, Dino and I have spent Christmas at my parents' villa and have gone to mass with them. Naturally on the fifth and sixth of January we've celebrated Epiphany. Dino has put out his stocking for La Befana to fill with candy. He hasn't known anything different, but thanks to you a new tradition has been started."

"Because of me?"

"Yes. You answered his letter, and a whole new world of hope has opened up for him. Dino is like any child who will keep taking more and more. But this experience hasn't been fair to you because you know what's involved and I can see that it's almost impossible for you to say no to him about anything. That's my fault. I'm just as bad and I've selfishly allowed and urged it."

"No, Luca. Not selfishly. You've lived for the last two years not wanting to say no to him. I don't know how you've handled everything. In the short time I've known him, I can tell you I've wanted to be here for him every bit as much. When Edda asked me if I would like to take him a gift, I leaped at the chance."

"I'm thankful you did. Dino's not the only one happy that you've come into his life, but you already know that."

"The feeling's mutual." She could hear her voice throb. "Would it be possible for me to see a video of Dino's famous *papà* winning the gold medal? Dino says it's in the family room. I'd love to see you doing the sport you love so much. I know I heard about you winning when I was around sixteen."

"You don't want to see that."

"I do. Please—" She stared into his eyes.

"Then come with me."

Filled with excitement, she followed him through the villa to the family room and sat down on the couch while he found the disc and put it in the machine.

Then he joined her and put his arm around her shoulders. For the next fifteen minutes she watched in utter disbelief to see him in the start house waiting for the signal. Then he flew down that mountain with unmatchable skill and beat every other competitor's time.

He'd been drop-dead gorgeous at twenty-two, but ten years later he was even more attractive. His white devastating smile combined with his bronzed olive complexion melted her to the core. As he accepted the gold medal to the accompaniment of the Italian national anthem, tears came to her eyes and melted her to the core of her being.

She turned to him. "How absolutely fabulous, Luca. I'm so proud of you. Don't tell me it wasn't the most exciting moment of your entire life!"

"One of them," he confessed.

"I saw your mother hugging you after. Where was your father?"

"He didn't come because he hated my love of skiing."

Her eyes closed tightly for a moment. "I can't comprehend that."

"It doesn't matter."

Oh, Luca. "Of course it does. When I think of my father… He was so wonderful to me. Last night I told you about one miracle that happened to my friend after we wished on a star. But I experienced an even greater miracle when I was seven. My father was going to die, so I talked to the priest and asked him to ask God to make him better. The priest told me to go home and ask God myself.

"I was very upset by this, but I did what he said. Only two days after I prayed to God to help my dying father, he started to get better and lived until three years ago. It was a great miracle."

"Those are experiences you'll never forget in your whole life. As far as I'm concerned, your coming to the villa to see Dino has constituted another one. Especially being here with me tonight."

He lowered his head and started kissing her again. Gabi feared getting more involved with this unforgettable man. The awful possibility that his feelings for her might not last caused her to pull away from him. "I can't do this, Luca."

She stood up, afraid to look him in the eyes. "On the drive here yesterday, I determined to help any way I can. Until he's had the operation, I'll avail myself as much as possible to help make him secure. Edda knows the situation and will give me the time off I need. But to get any more involved with you right now—"

"We *are* involved," he said in a grating voice and got to his feet. "But for the time being, we'll concentrate on Dino. To know you'll be there for him through the surgery will help him and save my sanity."

"You can count on me, Luca. I wouldn't be anywhere else. What I'm going to do is have a talk with Edda when I get back to work on Monday morning. Maybe midweek, say Wednesday, I could be here when Dino gets home from school."

"He'll be thrilled."

"If you made arrangements for Paolo to

come home with him, we could have a fun day and evening. It would give Dino something to look forward to. How would you feel about that?"

"I'll contact Paolo's parents as soon as you get permission from Edda. Even if he can't come, Dino will be overjoyed to see you before next weekend."

"As soon as I know on Monday, I'll call you."

He stood there with his powerful legs slightly apart. "There are no words to thank you, Gabi."

She got to her feet. "You don't have to thank me. Dino is a blessing in my life, too. If I can play any part in answering your son's prayer, nothing could make me happier."

"Where did you come from?" he asked quietly.

"I've found myself asking the same question about you. One day I'd love to hear how Luca Berettini became all the things he is, but not tonight. I can see you're exhausted. *Buona notte.*"

CHAPTER SIX

LUCA WONDERED IF he was dreaming when he heard, "Papà?" He turned over and opened his eyes. No. He hadn't been dreaming. Had Dino awakened with a nightmare? Here he'd just told Gabi his son had been free of them for the last few days.

He shot up in bed. "What's wrong?"

"Nothing. I just wanted you to get up and show me how to stuff a *corneto* with jam for Gabi's breakfast and serve her in bed. I'm afraid I'll make a mess. Can you fix her cappuccino, too?"

Relief washed over him in waves. "You want to bring it upstairs to her room?"

"*Si.* Paolo's *mamma* is going to have a baby and his *papà* took her breakfast in bed."

"I see." Luca chuckled. "What kind of jam did you have in mind?"

"Frutti di bosco."

"Tell you what. Let's both get dressed, then we'll hurry down to the kitchen and get busy."

"Fantastico!"

Within a half hour, they arrived at her door with a tray. Luca held it while Dino knocked. "Gabi? Are you awake?"

"Yes."

"Can I come in?"

"Of course!"

"My *papà* is with me."

"Oh—"

Luca smiled.

"Just a second, Dino."

His son looked up at him while they waited.

"You can come in now."

Dino opened the door. Luca's gaze focused on the gorgeous woman who'd just come out of the bathroom in bare feet wearing a knee-length pale blue robe. She didn't need makeup. He loved her tousled hair.

"*Buongiorno, signora.* We've brought your breakfast I made myself. I mean… I made part of it."

"You did all this for me?" Dino nodded. "Well, aren't I the luckiest person on the planet. *Grazie.*"

"*Prego.* Where would you like us to put it?"

"Right over there on the table in front of the window. We can all eat together and enjoy the view. I'll pull up the dressing table chair so there are seats for the three of us."

Luca couldn't stop staring at her. "Dino wanted to surprise you."

"It's the best surprise I ever had. This *corneto* is superb. You say you made it yourself?"

"I didn't cook it. Papà showed me how to put the jam in the middle."

"Well, you did a perfect job and it's absolutely delicious. I'm totally impressed. What did I do to deserve having breakfast served in my room?"

Luca could tell his son had something specific on his mind, but he had no idea what it was.

"I think we should talk about a new job for you."

Both she and Luca choked on their coffee and reached for a napkin from the tray. "A *new* one?" she murmured.

"*Si.* I know you have to work, so I wish you could be my new *mamma*."

Luca wasn't at all surprised. Out of the mouths of babes…

Gabi said, "You already have Ines. But I can come to see you whenever possible."

"But if you were my *mamma*, you'd live right here."

"True, but Edda has hired me to work for her. I couldn't just leave her."

His expression sobered. "Wouldn't you rather be my *mamma* than work for her?"

Before Luca could try to salvage the situation, she said, "I tell you what. I'll have a talk with her about taking a vacation so I can be with you more."

"You will?"

"Yes."

"Evviva."

Gabi was a master psychologist. Without promising Dino anything, she'd bought some time. But knowing his son, Dino would plague her for an answer every time he was with her. While they were finishing their breakfast, Luca's cell phone rang. It was his mother, wanting to know if she and his father could come over. Luca told her he'd call her back in a few minutes and hung up. His son had just finished the last of his *corneto.*

"Dino? Your *nonni* wants to drop by for a visit."

He frowned. "You mean today?"

With that one word Luca already had his answer. "Yes."

"But Gabi's here and we're going to play. They'll probably stay a long time and she has to go back to Padova later."

His son had a point and Luca had no desire to see his father, who probably wouldn't be impressed by Dino's attachment to Gabi. "All right. We'll make it for another day. Right now, why don't we go downstairs so she can get dressed."

Dino brightened and stood up. "Don't take too long, Gabi. We'll be in the family room."

"I promise I'll hurry."

Luca put their plates and cups back on the tray and carried it out the door. Dino followed him after giving Gabi a hug, and they walked down to the kitchen. His son darted to the family room, giving Luca time to phone his mother and tell her that Dino wanted Gabi all to himself for the day.

"I never thought I'd see the day he'd become this close to another woman. Maria and Tomaso can't believe it either. When they call him, Gabi is all he talks about. It's like it happened overnight!" his mother exclaimed.

"She has a special way with her. It's why she works for the foundation."

"Your father's not pleased. He still wants you to meet up with Giselle."

"That's too bad. I have never been interested in Giselle. He needs to give up that fiction."

"I know you wanted nothing to do with her, but he can't seem to let it go and is upset about Gabi spending so much time with Dino."

"Well, I'm not. *Grazie al cielo* you sent his letter. Dino is so happy right now, Gabi is exactly what he needs leading up to the operation."

"But what's going to happen afterward? She has her own life to lead."

Luca closed his eyes for a moment. He knew what he wanted but kept his thoughts to himself. "I can't answer that. No one can. It's all I can do to hold it together for the next two weeks."

"I realize that. Let me know how I can help."

"You do it all the time, and I love you for it. I'll talk to you later." They hung up.

Luca especially couldn't control Dino, who had a strong mind and will of his own. His son was determined to keep Gabi close no matter how he manipulated to get his way. Luca's mother would be shocked if she'd heard Dino say he wanted Gabi for his mother. But he couldn't blame Dino for anything, not when Luca was already imagining Gabi in his life on a permanent basis.

On his way to the family room, Luca heard laughter. Gabi had kept her promise to get dressed fast. Already they were involved in some game. When he walked in, Dino ran up to him.

"Look what Gabi brought me! She has a collection of her favorite *Tex* comic books and says I can keep them for as long as I want. Come and read with us."

Luca hadn't thought Gabi could do anything else to enchant his son, but he'd been wrong. Their connection really was uncanny. His eyes shot to hers. They were a beautiful green with flecks of gold. Right now they revealed the depth of her emotions brought out by desires they were both having to hold in check.

The next time Luca got her alone…

After he took a deep breath, he said, "I think if we're going to read them, we should go in the living room. I'll light a fire and we'll get comfortable."

"I'll bring the snacks." Gabi picked up the box of chocolate insects.

Dino's expression crumpled, causing Luca's laughter to echo all the way through the villa. While his son lay on the floor poring over some of the comics for a little while, Gabi sat back on one end of the couch. Luca chose the other.

"Would you be willing to show me the new ski boots and skis you've designed?"

Luca flashed Gabi a wicked grin, reminding her of last night when they couldn't get enough of each other. "I'd rather see some more of your sketches. I know Edda needs you, but wouldn't it be exciting if you had a chance to go to art school and carve out a new career for yourself?"

"Of course it would."

Luca would have explored the possibility more, but then Dino wanted to put a puzzle together. Afterward they ate, then played another round of cops and robbers. Until the grandfather clock chimed the half hour, Luca forgot what it was like not to have a worry in the world.

Gabi lifted her head. "I can't believe it's three thirty already. I'm afraid I'm going to have to leave for Padova."

"Not yet," Dino protested.

"It's a long drive," Luca reminded him, hating for this to happen after such a glorious day.

"I don't want to go either, Dino, but it'll be dark before I get home and I have a lot to do to get ready for work in the morning."

He jumped up. "You said you would talk to your boss."

She tousled his hair. "I will."

Luca groaned silently before darting her a glance. "Are you packed?"

"Yes."

"Then I'll bring your case down. Come and help me, Dino."

"While you do that, I'll clean up the living room and put everything back in the family room."

Anyone watching them would describe it as a scene of domestic bliss set on the cover of a Christmas card. But that would be without seeing the turmoil going on inside Luca, who couldn't bear to be parted from Gabi.

Gabi put on her coat while Dino insisted on carrying her case out to the car and putting it in the backseat. Some of the snow had melted, but not all. There'd be more coming in the next few days. Luca would give anything for Gabi not to have to drive in it.

She got inside behind the wheel and lowered the window when Luca and Dino walked around. "Thank you for the loveliest weekend I've ever had. Be good in school, Dino, and send me an email telling me what project you're working on this next week."

"I will. Let me know when you've talked to Edda."

Her eyes sent Luca a silent message. "I promise."

"Drive safely," he whispered. Suddenly the thought of anything happening to her filled him with such terror he could hardly breathe. A car accident on the black ice of the highway could end her life as fast as the avalanche that had buried Catarina. Even thinking about that possibility made him realize he'd fallen in love with Gabi.

After losing Catarina, the pain had been so terrible, he'd never wanted to care like that about another woman again. Yet here he was, frightened to lose this woman who'd become of vital importance to him in every way. He simply couldn't go through that kind of pain again.

"Text me when you get home so we can stop worrying."

She nodded.

"When you're on vacation, you won't have to drive from Padova." Dino never gave up. "You've got your own room at our villa and Pia will make all your food. Can your *mamma* drive?" Luca wasn't surprised at the question. His enterprising son worked all the angles.

"Si." She smiled at Luca.

"Then she can come and visit, can't she, Papà?"

"Of course."

"*A piu' tardi*," Gabi said before she started down the drive to the road leading into town.

Dino left his side on a run and dashed inside the villa. The only thing saving Luca was Gabi's promise to come midweek. He was already living for it.

Before Gabi had driven away, she'd seen anxiety in Luca's eyes. It matched hers. She knew he didn't like it that she had to drive so far, especially after it had snowed. The thought of an accident haunted her, too. Worse, they were both suffering from a new burden Dino had placed on her.

To her relief she got home safely. The second she turned off the engine, she texted Luca. Almost immediately he texted back, thrilling her.

We miss you. I'm going to be as bad as Dino and remind you to get back to me when you can about plans for midweek.

She pressed a hand to her heart. That was all she'd been thinking about.

I'll text you tomorrow after my talk with Edda.

Don't write anything else, Gabi, or he's going to know you're head over heels in love with him.

Gabi dashed in the house. "Mamma?"

"Oh, good. You're home. I take it you had a wonderful time."

"You can't imagine."

"I think I can."

"I want to hear about your weekend with Angelina."

"Since you've been with Dino's dashing father for the weekend, I'm afraid anything I have to say isn't worth mentioning."

"That's not true!"

Her mother's laughter followed Gabi, who carried her suitcase down the hall to her bedroom. Before she did anything else, she sat down at her computer to send an email to Dino. She'd promised.

Wednesday morning Luca drove Dino to school and dropped him off. "I'll see you at one o'clock."

"Do you promise Gabi is coming this afternoon?"

"Do I have to? You read her email. She's excited to meet Paolo."

"But—"

"But what?"

"I don't know."

"Dino—she's coming! See you in a little while." His son climbed out of the rear seat and hurried inside the building with his backpack.

Luca sped to work, grateful there hadn't been fresh snow yet to become a hazard for Gabi. He would put in a few hours, needing to keep busy until he went back to the villa to welcome Gabi. She planned to be there by one thirty.

Around eleven that morning, while he was dictating some letters to his secretary, he got a text from Gabi. At first his heart almost failed him. Until he read it.

I left Padova early. Will be at the villa by twelve thirty.

From that point on he was out of breath. After clearing his desk of work, he told his secretary he was leaving for the day and took off for Maniago. He'd planned for Gabi to stay overnight and drive back to Padova early Thursday morning for work. The cook had instructions to fix meals the boys would love.

Luca walked out the front entrance when he saw Gabi's car pull up the drive. She slid from the driver's seat wearing another long-sleeved sweater, this time in a bright blue with a navy skirt. With the fifty-eight-degree temperature, she obviously didn't feel the need to wear a coat. The silvery ash of her blond hair combined with her curvaceous figure robbed him of breath.

"You got here early!"

Her smile knocked him sideways. "Edda told me to leave. I was hoping I would be on time so I could go with you to pick up the boys. I'd love to see Dino's school."

"He'll be ecstatic when he finds out you're with me. Do you want to freshen up before we leave?"

"I'm fine."

"Then come and get in my car."

After she locked her car with the remote, he cupped her elbow and helped her in the Lancia. Before he started the engine, his gaze wandered over her. He loved the strawberry fragrance drifting from her hair. "I've read your emails with Dino, but I want to know how you've really been."

"Probably the same as you. Thank goodness we only have to hold out nine more days until he goes in the hospital."

He nodded. "Having Paolo come over has given him something new to think about."

"That's good."

"Paolo's parents will come and get him after dinner. Dino's happy about that because he doesn't want to share you with Paolo into the night." She let out a gentle laugh. "You think I'm kidding, but I'm not. I can't say I blame him. There's no act to follow you."

"Luca..."

"It's true. My whole household has undergone a distinct shift since Gabi Parisi arrived bearing gifts in answer to a certain letter."

Gabi's eyes filmed over. "My life has changed, too. You have to know that. He's the sweetest boy in the world. How lucky he is to have you for his father."

"Thank you," he whispered before pulling her to him. "I've missed you, Gabi."

"I've missed you, too."

He kissed her long and hard, unable to wait another second to feel her in his arms. But it was time to leave for the school before he forgot where they were and he started to devour her where anyone could see them. After letting her go, he turned on the engine and drove down to the road.

"You live in a virtual garden even though its winter."

"I love it and run along here most mornings at six."

"Does Dino ever join you?"

"He'll need the doctor's permission first because he doesn't want his head jarred. When that happens he'll probably keep up for about a block and then quit."

"He loves you so much. One day he'll be well again."

"I need to believe that." Needing more contact, Luca reached over and grasped her hand. "You give me hope anything is possible."

"That's because it is. Try not to dwell on what will happen after the tumor is removed." She squeezed his hand before letting it go, leaving him bereft.

Before long they entered the town. Luca drove to the piazza with the fountain and parked on the east side. Dino's school building was one of several surrounding it.

"This must be a fun place for the children to enjoy."

"The school uses it for parades and plays. The rest of the time it's a playground." He shut off the engine and turned toward her. They still had a few minutes before Dino came out. Luca craved every second he could be alone with her and studied her profile.

Her gaze darted to him. She couldn't keep his eyes off him either. "Have you always lived in Maniago?"

"I was born and raised here."

"What about Dino's mother?"

Oddly enough any questions about her didn't bother him anymore. Naturally Gabi wanted, needed, to know about her in order to have normal conversations with Dino.

"Sorry, Luca. I—"

"Don't be sorry," he broke in on her. "Ask me anything you want. It doesn't hurt me to talk about her. In fact, I think it's good that we do. We both know Dino is afraid to have the operation because Catarina isn't here. But if he wants to talk about her, he should feel free to do so and so should you."

She nodded. "Was Catarina from Maniago, too?"

"No. Venice."

"That city is one of my favorite places to explore and sketch. I drive there when I can, often with my mother. Does Dino love it, too?"

"I haven't taken him there since the avalanche. In the beginning, it pained me too much to consider making the trip."

"Of course it would." Gabi eyed him intently. "Does Dino have grandparents there on his mother's side?"

"No. Catarina's parents died when she was in her teens, so her aunt and uncle Maria and Tomaso Guardino raised her along with their own two children. He works for our company and commutes from Venice. That's how I met

Catarina. They've come to visit Dino many times. He enjoys them both."

"So *they're* the couple I've seen in some of the little photos in Dino's room."

He nodded.

"I can't imagine losing Dino's mother the way you did," she said.

"It was horrific, but what would have made it worse was to lose Dino, too."

She shook her head. "Was there no warning?"

"Yes. A crack, like the loudest thunder you've ever heard in your life. It shook the ground and reverberated throughout the entire valley. I knew what it meant because I'd lived through several avalanches both in France and Austria.

"In an instant I picked up Dino and shouted to Catarina that we had to get off the mountain now. But we still couldn't move out of the way fast enough. This one came shooting down with the speed of sound and swallowed everything before you could even think. We were buried alive and I had to swim through it, trying to hold on to Dino.

"The ski patrol had to dig down through ten feet to find my wife's body. I'd swum near the top of the cascading snow with Dino in order to ride it out. There was no way I could have found her."

Gabi shuddered. "No wonder he has nightmares."

"He's not the only one."

She reached out to touch his arm. "Edda heard about it on the news and said Dino got injured."

"That's right. Somehow the tip of my ski pole punctured his scalp."

"Oh, Luca—I can't believe it."

"Neither could I. You probably know the rest. The wound healed, but the X-rays they took showed a tumor of all things and another nightmare began. The doctor felt it best to wait for an operation until he turned seven."

She shook her head. "I don't know why some people are forced to live through so much tragedy. I can't comprehend it. Edda told me it made the world news for days, but that was at the time when I was going through a divorce and wasn't aware of anything else."

"Which is understandable."

"There are degrees of pain, Luca. Yours has to be the worst. I'm so sorry for what happened to you. Your poor families. All the agony and suffering you've gone through while you've been waiting for Dino to have the operation."

He covered her hand still touching his arm. "You've been through agony, too. My friend Giles, a ski buddy, got divorced recently. He said it's worse than death."

"It felt that way to me, too, at first, but no longer."

"Ever since Dino told me you'd been married, I've wanted to ask you about it, but we haven't had time alone to talk like this before now. My son would monopolize your time every second if he could. Half the time I have to fight to get a word in."

She laughed.

"He said you'd wanted children."

"I did. What I didn't tell him was that I had a miscarriage before I learned Santos had been unfaithful to me."

"*Gabi—*" He reached across the seat to cup her neck. "I had no idea."

"We'd only been married ten months, but it didn't matter. I filed for divorce and moved back with my mother."

"You've had so much pain with his betrayal, I don't know how you've survived it. I want to hear more, but if you look out the window right now, you'll see our time is up because it appears school has ended."

Luca had been so involved in their conversation, the boys had almost reached them without his being aware of anything. Quickly he levered himself from the driver's seat. But Dino only had eyes for their visitor.

"Gabi—"

She got out and was almost knocked over by the hug he gave her. "I thought I'd come and surprise you. This must be Paolo."

"Buongiorno, signora."

Dino's friend, who was an inch shorter with chestnut-colored hair, was on his best behavior for the moment, but he could get rambunctious. His mother must have had a talk with him. Luca could only wonder how long it would last.

"It's so nice to meet you, Paolo. I've heard you're a good swimmer. I can't wait to watch both of you in the water one day."

Trust Gabi to say something to make everyone feel better. There was no one like her.

"Papà says I swim like a tadpole."

"That wouldn't surprise me, Dino."

Luca put a hand on their shoulders. "What do you say we get in the car and go home for lunch."

"Cook is making us pizza!" Dino announced as they drove home.

Gabi looked over her shoulder. "We have some special snacks for Paolo, don't we, Dino?"

Luca started to chuckle. He couldn't help it.

Nonstop commentary continued from the backseat to the villa. Once Dino dragged Gabi's suitcase into the house, they all headed for the bathroom to wash up. Then they sat down at the table to eat.

Halfway through the meal Luca's phone rang. He'd told his secretary not to call unless it was an emergency. Maybe it was his mother. When he checked the caller ID, it surprised him to see that Dr. Meuller was phoning. For some reason it unnerved him. The neurosurgeon was supposed to be in Kenya right now.

Luca looked at Gabi, who eyed him with concern. "Excuse me. I've got to take this call, but I'll be right back."

After getting up from the table, he hurried into the living room and clicked On. "Dr. Meuller?"

"Hello, Luca. How is my patient?"

"Remarkably well all things considered." All of it due to Gabi.

"That's good news. I have some, too. My work here in Nairobi finished up sooner than I'd anticipated. What I'd like to do is move up Dino's operation a week. Would that be possible for you?"

His hand tightened on the phone. "You mean *this* coming Saturday?"

"This Friday actually. You'll have to be at the hospital by six in the morning."

That was the day after tomorrow!

CHAPTER SEVEN

"IF THAT WON'T work for you, I understand. I haven't given you much notice."

"No, no. I'm thrilled with this news. The sooner you remove that tumor, the sooner my son won't get those headaches anymore. We'll be there Friday morning on the dot."

"Excellent. I'll make all the arrangements so the staff is ready for you when you check in."

"Thank you, Doctor. See you soon."

Luca hung up in a daze. After two years, the operation they'd been waiting for was really going to happen! He needed to inform his work that he was going to be out of the office for an unknown period of time. Before the day was out, Dino's teacher would have to be told he might not be back to school until after the new year. The doctor couldn't give him a timetable for a full recovery. Luca refused to believe Dino wouldn't be cured.

But most important of all, he had to tell Gabi what was happening and ask—beg her if necessary—to take the time off to be with them. Luca would call Edda Romano and explain why it was so vital Gabi had to be there for Dino. Luca couldn't imagine getting through this experience without her.

He knew it was a lot to ask. Too much. Luca realized it depended on how much she loved Dino. She *did* love him. Luca had seen it and felt it in a dozen ways.

After calling his mother, who would alert Maria and Tomaso that the timetable for the operation had changed, he phoned the school to leave a message with Dino's teacher. Once he'd hung up, he followed the children's excited voices to the family room. Gabi was playing charades with them, acting out a movie or book title. She exchanged a secret glance with Luca while he stood there and watched for a few minutes.

What would life be like a week from today? A month? He didn't have an answer for that. What he did know was that there would be a huge change and he had to be ready for it no matter what. If Gabi only knew she was the magic dust to help them navigate through the uncharted section of their universe.

They played a few more charades before she said, "You're both tied for first place! Dino? If you'll bring my suitcase in here, I have prizes to give out."

"Evviva!" He was off and back like a shot.

"Put it here on the couch."

The boys clustered around her as she opened the lid and pulled out two Christmas-wrapped boxes the size of a big game. They took up most of the suitcase. At this point, Luca's excitement to see what she'd brought them was greater than theirs.

Within seconds they'd ripped off the paper and out flew twin Roman gladiator outfits: brown tunics, arm shields, armor, swords, daggers, axes and helmets with red gladiator feathers on top. But there was more. Each box contained a bag of fifty small Roman soldiers so they could play war.

No doubt about it. She'd broken the bank with these gifts. Luca didn't need to remind his son to thank her.

Dino flung himself at her and clung. "*Ti amo*, Gabi." The love in his voice was so tangible, you could pick it up where it had dripped onto the area rug covering the slate tiles. Paolo lifted a beaming face to her. "*Grazie mille*, Gabi."

She gave them both a hug. "I want you to get dressed up so I can take your pictures." While they hustled to do her bidding, she pulled the phone out of her pocket and started snapping photos.

"Woo-hoo!" she cried out. "You guys look terrific. Why don't you run to the kitchen? Pia and Ines won't know who you are."

"Come on!" Dino called to Paolo, and they ran out of the family room holding their weapons.

She turned to Luca. "Now that they're gone for a minute, tell me what caused that sudden dark expression to break out on your face earlier."

Gabi didn't miss much. "It was Dr. Meuller."

Her eyes grew anxious. "Is something wrong?"

"No. But he has come home sooner than planned and is going to do the operation on Friday morning."

"*This* Friday?" she murmured, visibly shocked.

"It means he has to be there by six in the morning." He had trouble swallowing. "Gabi—"

"I know what you're going to say," she interrupted him. "For the operation to happen this soon instead of a week from now, naturally you're facing this moment you've been worrying sick over and now it's become real."

Grim lines broke out on his face. "Anything could go wrong. Dino's life could be altered. He might not be able to have the normal life I've wanted for him, or worse."

"Don't go there, Luca."

Without thinking what he was doing, he reached for her and pulled her into his arms, burying his face in her hair. "I can't do this without you."

She lifted her head and stared into his eyes. "You won't have to. Don't worry. I'll talk to Edda. She'll understand I have to be here for him. I want to be here for him and you. I love him."

"There's no doubt how he feels about you. His declaration moments ago said it all."

"He's so precious."

"So are you," Luca whispered against her lips before urging them apart. He needed this more than he needed air to breathe and started drinking from her mouth. He'd been waiting to know this kind of rapture again. Her passionate response only fueled his hunger. His world reeled as her body melted into his like she was made for him. He couldn't resist caressing her back and womanly hips, unable to get enough of this marvelous, giving woman.

Gabi must have heard the patter of feet before he did. By the time the boys burst into the family room, she'd eased herself away from him. But her breath was coming in short spurts and her lips looked swollen.

She could tell the shape he was in and had the presence of mind to start cleaning up the wrapping paper strewn over the rug. "Did you scare Ines?"

"No, but Pia screamed."

Both Luca and Gabi laughed. "Come on over to the table and set up your army, *ragazzi*. Then we'll have a great war."

"*Si!*" they shouted in a collective voice.

Luca decided she could have been the original Pied Piper. When they were all ready to play, she eyed Dino. "Why don't you give Paolo a snack."

Dino flashed her an impish grin that caught at Luca's heart. His son hurried over to the bookcase with the red feathers bobbing on the top of his helmet. Then he put the open box of chocolate insects next to his friend. A few were missing.

"Cioccolato!" Paolo bit into one of the worms. "Mmm. It's pretty good."

When he'd eaten it, Dino broke down laughing. "Look what he did, Papà."

Luca nodded. "Don't you think it's time you had one, too? Gabi was so nice to bring them."

"I know."

"Gladiators loved them," she teased. "But it doesn't matter if you don't want one."

To his surprise her gentle goading forced Dino to reach for a worm and eat it. There was nothing like a little peer pressure, too.

Gabi clapped. *"Bravo!"*

"Hey—that wasn't bad."

Thanks to Gabi, this was a great victory for Dino. Luca was proud of him and hoped it was a good omen to overcome his fear for the operation.

The boys settled down to a game of war, then everyone got busy finishing the building blocks project. This was followed by a game of cops and robbers. By then dinner was ready. After they'd eaten, Paolo's parents came to get him. Already it was dark out.

Everyone assembled at the front door. "I had

the best time of my life!" he told his mother, still dressed in his costume.

No surprise there. He sounded just like Dino.

Paolo looked at Gabi. "Are you going to be here again?"

"Yes!" Dino answered for her. "*Ciao*, Paolo."

"*Ciao*, Dino. Thanks for the gladiator game, Gabi."

"You're so welcome. See you again soon."

"*Ciao*, Signor Berettini."

After Luca shut the door, they went back to the family room to clean up everything. Luca eyed his happy son, who was still dressed in his costume. It had been another perfect day. "Guess what?"

"I know. I have to get ready for bed." They started up the stairs. "I wish you didn't have to go back to Padova in the morning."

"We've had this discussion before, *figlio mio*. Come on. I'll run your bath."

Gabi took advantage of the time to freshen up in the guest bedroom. Then she called her mother to tell her about the change in plans for Dino.

"I need to phone Edda and tell her what's

happened, but I think I'm just going to stay here until the operation is over. I've packed enough things to last me for a few days. It seems ridiculous to drive all the way home for more clothes just to come back again."

"I agree. While you're in Padova for the operation, you can drop by the house for anything else you need. If you want my opinion, this time change for the operation is a good thing."

"I know it is. Luca has been on a countdown for too long."

"The situation has been hard on you, too, darling."

"You can hardly compare two weeks of worry to two years." She let out a deep sigh. "Today he told me about the avalanche. It was so horrific, I don't know how he has functioned since. He's a remarkable man, Mamma."

She shared some of things she'd learned with her mother. "I'd love to talk longer, but I need to get in touch with Edda."

"Go ahead and call her. We'll stay in close touch."

"I love you. Thank you for always being there."

She hung up and phoned her boss. Edda answered and was absolutely wonderful about everything. "That child needs you to cling to. Your presence will represent all of us from the foundation. You know our prayers will be with him, his doctor, his father and everyone who loves him."

"Thank you, Edda. I'll say it again. You're a saint. *Buona notte.* I'll keep you posted around the clock."

Gabi got off the phone and was reduced to tears. The relief of knowing the operation was coming a week sooner had opened the floodgates. She loved Dino like he was her own son.

For so long she felt like she'd been walking on eggshells, trying to do the right thing, hoping she didn't say or do the wrong thing. And all the time she'd been falling hopelessly in love with Luca, who was facing an uncertain future once the operation was over. Gabi's future was uncertain, too. The fear of losing Luca once everything was over had grabbed hold of her.

After forcing herself to calm down, she went into the bathroom once more to wash her face and brush her hair. Then she hurried down the hall to Dino's bedroom. The door was open. Luca sat on the side of the bed while his son knelt to finish saying his prayers. "…

and please bless Edda that she'll let Gabi have a vacation."

After hearing his heartfelt plea, Gabi tiptoed in the room and sat down next to Luca, who put his arm around her waist, filling her with warmth. When Dino lifted his head, she said, "I just talked to Edda."

"You did?"

"Yes. She's giving me time off so I can spend it with you."

"When?"

"Starting right now."

He blinked. "For how long?"

Luca squeezed her side. "For as long as you need me."

"So you don't have to leave?"

"No. How does that sound?"

She could tell it was a lot for him to take in. He looked at his father. "What do you think, Papà?"

"I think it sounds wonderful."

"So do I!" He leaped to his feet and threw his arms around her neck.

Luca stood up. "You still have to go to school in the morning," he reminded him. "Come on. Climb under the covers."

Gabi smiled down at him. "I liked Paolo."

"More than me?"

"What do you mean, more than you?" She tickled him until he was laughing. "I couldn't love any boy the way I love you. Now it's time to go to sleep. See you in the morning."

"Promise you'll be here?"

She was beginning to realize what Luca had been living through for the last two years. Everything you said and did with Dino meant life and death to him because he'd seen his mother vanish before his very eyes, never to come back. It was not hard to understand Luca's burden. He had no idea what was going to happen once Dino came back from that operating room.

"I promise." She kissed his forehead and left the room.

Gabi knew she couldn't sleep yet, so she went downstairs to the living room. Luca followed her and stoked up the fire. Then he sat down on the couch next to her where they could feel its warmth.

She turned to him. "What kind of tumor does he have?"

"It's called an astrocytoma, a slow-growing, noncancerous tumor that is usually found in children from five to eight."

"I see. If there'd been no avalanche, how would you have known about the tumor?"

"He would have eventually manifested several symptoms, with headaches being the most obvious."

"What will his surgery be like?"

"The doctor said he'll perform a keyhole craniotomy. In other words, it's a minimally invasive surgical procedure. Dino is a good candidate for it because his skull-based tumor is in a good location.

"They go in behind the ear where there's little scarring. The doctor said there's less pain and a faster recovery time. The downside, of course, is the danger of disturbing tissue around it. The more precise he can be in removing it, the better."

"Has he given you an idea of how long Dino will be in the hospital?"

Luca rubbed the back of his neck, a gesture she'd seen once before at his most vulnerable. "If all goes well, he could be home in three days. Some children go right back to school if there are no complications. Others have to be watched for several weeks or months. The doctor said every case is different, but most children bounce back faster than adults."

"Then we'll just have to pray that happens. I'm not going to think about what could go wrong. That doesn't help any of us."

He stared at her. "One of these days Edda will know my gratitude for sharing you."

She smiled at him. "I talked to my mother, too. She's a nurse and will do anything she can to help. So—" Gabi put her hands on her knees, "I'm here to stay for as long as you believe Dino needs me around."

"How about for as long as *I* need you? When you're with me, I feel like I can cope."

"That's a very touching compliment, but it's also a huge responsibility. Will it help if I assure you I'm not going anywhere?"

"I'll take you any way I can get you."

She laughed, but with those words her heart had started to thud. He hadn't told her he loved her. What if he never did? How would she be able to bear it?

"In case you were wondering, I've enjoyed kissing you at every chance possible," he inserted, knowing exactly what was on her mind. "To be honest, I never wanted to stop. As for tonight, it was a good thing you heard the children beating a path back to the family room.

So I'm giving you fair warning. You're in big trouble if you get too close to me."

Luca didn't know it, but he was in danger from her. "I'm not worried."

"For all the reasons that my son is crazy about you, it seems I, too, have developed a crush on this amazing woman from Padova. To think she has a fascination for chocolate-covered insects and an addiction to cartoon heroes like Tex Willer! Who would have thought?"

Loving this man as she did, there were things she wanted desperately to know about him. "For Dino to have loved his mother so much, she had to be a very remarkable woman. Was Catarina your first love?"

"My first *real* love? Yes. First attraction, no. From the age of twenty to twenty-five, I competed on the Italian national ski team and met a lot of women. After placing first and second at the Olympic trials, I made the Italian Olympic team. It wasn't until after I gave it up and went into the family business that I met Catarina."

"Was she a skier, too?"

"No. I tried to teach her, but she wasn't crazy about it. What about you? Have you ever done any skiing?"

"No. None at all. That probably sounds crazy to you, but I never had an opportunity. My friends didn't ski either. How many medals have you actually won?"

"I was only in the Olympics one year and brought home the gold medal for the downhill. But if you're talking about awards, I won a lot during the years I was on the Italian ski team."

"Where are they?"

"In storage."

"Your gold medal, too?"

"Yes." That explained why his son hadn't shown the medal to her by now. "I already sold the family chalet in Piancavallo so he never has to be reminded of what happened there."

Gabi could understand Luca avoiding the place where disaster had struck. Skiing hadn't been a part of life with his son since the avalanche. Maybe he'd train his son to be an Olympic swimmer.

While she was deep in thought, he got up from the couch and turned to her. "Do you know we never talk about you and your life? It's always about me. Are you still in so much pain over your divorce, you can't talk about it?

Do you still love the man you married? Where is your ex-husband now? Is Parisi your married name, or your family name?"

She stood up. "Luca—we'll talk about me another time."

His eyes never left hers. "In ways, I feel I know you through Dino. He's dropped little pieces of information here and there. Just enough to tease me. Why didn't you pursue a career in art? Is that why you love Venice so much? Did you only own one dog? I'm planning to get Dino a dog after his operation.

"The more we're together, the more I realize I don't really know you at all or how you ended up working for Edda Romano. But what is evident is that my son has bonded with you, and I thank God you relieved him of a great worry tonight after he said his prayers. It also relieved me because I'm going to need you tomorrow when I tell him he has to go to the hospital on Friday."

Gabi nodded. "I've been thinking about that, too."

"Shall I bring it up tomorrow night at bedtime, or earlier? What does your intuition tell you?"

She paced the floor for a minute. "I should

think the less time he has to worry about it, the better."

"Then we'll do it together before he says his prayers."

She wanted to wrap her arms around him and tell him everything was going to be all right, but a drawn expression had broken out on his handsome features, causing an ache in her heart. Now wasn't the right time.

"I'll go on up and see you in the morning. I hope you'll be able to get some sleep tonight."

"I doubt there'll be much sleep for either of us," his voice grated.

Gabi hurried out of the living room to the family room to get her suitcase and take it upstairs. She passed Dino's room but didn't hear a sound. It had to be a good sign he was asleep.

In a few minutes she climbed into bed, but her mind was reeling from all the questions Luca had raised about her, questions she never knew he wanted answered. He hadn't brought them up until tonight, but he was so distressed and preoccupied, she imagined he was on the phone right now, needing to talk to his mother. Gabi realized that Giustina had been the one he'd turned to in order to cope all this time.

She tossed and turned during the night. When morning came, she was glad to get up and dressed. After putting on jeans and a cream-colored crew neck sweater with push-up sleeves to the elbow, she reached for her purse and hurried downstairs. Gabi heard Dino's voice coming from the kitchen and headed there.

As soon as he saw her, he ran over to hug her. He was dressed for school in his smock. "*Buongiorno*, Dino!" She hugged him hard. By this time tomorrow, he'd be in the hospital having the operation.

He put his head back and looked up at her with shining eyes. "I'm so glad you're here."

"So am I." This was a moment she needed to remember.

After lifting her head, she smiled at the cook and Ines before sitting down. "What a beautiful day! From my bedroom window I saw that the sun is out with no clouds. I can't believe it."

"I wish I didn't have to go to school."

"But think about all your friends who will be excited to see you. Especially Paolo."

"Gabi's right," his father's deep voice filled the kitchen.

"I guess."

Luca had been out running and was still wearing his navy sweats. There ought to be a law against a man who looked like a black-haired god from Olympus running around this early in the morning. It could give a woman a heart attack.

He sat down next to Dino. "Pia has made us a feast in Gabi's honor. You need to finish your breakfast so we can drive you to school."

Luca started eating as if there wasn't anything in the world troubling him. That helped Gabi, who ate another roll with her cappuccino before they headed out to the car. Dino brought his backpack and got in the backseat. She could get used to this life so fast it was scary. That's what was worrying her.

"Will you both pick me up right after school?" They'd stopped near the entrance. Gabi climbed out with Luca.

"What do you think?" He rubbed Dino's head. Gabi gave him another hug. "Where else would we be but right here?" Other kids were going inside. One of the girls waved to him.

"Who's that?" Gabi wanted to know.

"Filomena."

"Ah. She's cute. Maybe you should offer her one of the suckers in your backpack." Her suggestion produced a laugh that made his frown disappear.

"*A presto!*" Luca called to him.

When Dino had disappeared inside, they got back in the car. "Your son appears to be a normal Italian male. Already he's attracting the *ragazze*."

Luca laughed as they drove away from the piazza. To hear it warmed her heart. She noticed he hadn't taken the road back to the villa. "Where are we going?"

"Since you haven't been here before, I thought we'd take a drive through the hills to Tauriano. I'll show you my manufacturing plant where the skis and boots are made. It will give me time to hear more about your life. I want to know what the world was like for you in the beginning. We've got until one o'clock with nothing else to do."

"The beginning?"

"Yes. What was your legal name before you were married?"

"I was born Gabriella Russo. My childhood was idyllic. We lived in a small house in Limena on the outskirts of Padova. My father, Enrico, worked in business for the Constantini paper company."

"I know of it."

"My mother, Nadia, grew up in Padova and went to nursing school. Afterward she started work at a doctor's office where they met when Papà had to see the doctor."

"Was it love at first sight?"

She chuckled. "I think so. They got married fairly soon and moved into a little house. Before long I came along. There were lots of children in our neighborhood. We played all the time. I remember when one of my friends had some guinea pigs and we planned a marriage ceremony for them."

Luca laughed again and kept laughing as she told him her various antics. "As I told you earlier, when I was seven my father got sick with pneumonia and couldn't get better. I heard my mother tell her friend he might die. I loved him so much I was in agony. You know the rest. The priest told me to go home and ask for help myself. I got mad."

By now they'd reached the small town of Tauriano. Luca pulled in a lay-by that opened up into a fabulous view of the valley. He turned to her. "Why did you get mad?"

"Because I was afraid to do it myself, but somehow I found the courage."

"And history was written," he said in a soft voice.

Her eyes swam with tears. They always did that when she remembered what had transpired.

Luca pulled her over so she half lay against him. "I need to kiss you again, Gabi. You've become my addiction."

She responded with a hunger that surprised her because she'd been trying hard not to give in to her longings. But it was ridiculous to hold back, and he wouldn't let her anyway. They clung to each other, full of desire and the underlying emotions driving them.

"You're so beautiful," he murmured against her neck and throat. "You don't know what you do to me, what you mean to me."

"I feel the same way about you," she admitted. "In this whole world there's no one else like you."

Just as she'd said it, a car pulled into the lay-by behind them and some people got out. Luca groaned. "Wouldn't you know we couldn't have a moment's peace?"

Gabi straightened up and moved back on her side of the car. Luca started the engine, then grasped her hand and gave her a tour of the town. He drove them past the large two-story building with a sign that said Giulia.

"That's *your* trade name? I've seen it everywhere!"

He nodded. "I needed one unique word that would sell my product. It's identifiable as coming from the northeastern province of Italy, but I shortened the full name by cutting off Friuli-Venezia."

"I love it. Italian and original, just like you."

In the next breath he leaned over and kissed her even though people could see them. When he lifted his mouth, he said, "I'm not going to apologize for giving in to the impulse. I find myself wanting to do it constantly."

Heat filled her cheeks before he sat back and started driving again.

"Can we drive to Spilimbergo? I'd like to see where the big boss works."

"That's a good idea. When we get there I'll buy you a pizza *patate*. And en route I want to hear why you didn't pursue a career in art."

She shook her head. "That Dino has a lot to answer for."

"He absorbs information like a sponge, *if* he's interested."

Gabi chuckled. "Even though I had a part-time job, I'm afraid art school was too expensive and my father didn't make enough money to pay for it all. That was a disappointment because I liked to draw."

"That butterfly is a masterpiece."

"Hardly. But art school was out, and Papà urged me to try for a grant and go for something practical like an accounting degree. Businesses needed accountants, and it wouldn't cost so much."

"That was excellent advice."

"Needless to say I took it and ended up getting my degree. My father was very happy for me, but by then he'd developed heart problems and died of a fatal heart attack."

"Another difficult time for you."

She nodded. "I'm ashamed to say my faith wasn't very strong at that point."

"I hear you," Luca murmured. "Mine has been stretched many times. No one can measure the pain of another person's trial."

"That's true in theory. My mother helped me out until I could get an accounting job. I didn't know what I wanted to do and scanned the want ads. Nothing appealed because I was in a dark place.

"About then I found a temporary job at a

bank working as a teller while I waited for an accounting job to materialize. It was there I met Santos Parisi, manager of the bank. I fell hard for him. We got married four months later."

"That was fast."

"Too fast, and my happiness didn't last long once I'd suffered a miscarriage. One of the girls at the bank had seen Santos at a local club with another woman while he was supposed to be in Florence on business. She felt sorry for me because I was so recently married and thought I should know.

"When he got home I confronted him and found out he'd been with the woman he'd been having an affair with for a long time. He said it didn't mean anything and that he would give her up. But that was it for me. I'd been a fool."

"*He* was the fool, Gabi."

"Thank you for saying that. I moved out of our apartment and filed for divorce using any money I'd saved to pay the attorney fees."

"You've been through hell."

"That was a time when I thought the world was over for me. Then I saw there was an opening at the Start with a Wish foundation that helped children with problems realize a dream. I felt like a child myself, one who needed a dream to come true, so I applied. Since then life has been so much better."

"For Dino, too." Luca parked around the side of a café in Spilimbergo and kissed her again. "Thank you for confiding in me. Now I'm not quite so jealous of my son, who knows so many things about you I still have to learn. Wait here. I'll be right back."

A few minutes later he returned with the food he loved and gave her a piece. "I'm still full from breakfast and don't think I can eat all of it." But she was wrong and had finished it by the time Luca drove them by the Berettini Plastics Company, an enormous building.

"Even if you don't enjoy your work there, I'm impressed you can run two entirely different companies at the same time."

He sat back. "It's just work and I don't want to talk about me. Let's head back to the villa. I need a shower, then we'll pick up the new puzzle I ordered for Dino at the store before we reach his school. They only had one left."

"What kind of puzzle?"

"It's a thousand-piece cartoon version of building the Roman coliseum. I thought we'd set it up in the living room in front of the fire.

He'll love it, particularly since you bought him and Paolo those gladiator outfits. It has little figures of gladiators, soldiers, horses, plus workers and slaves. It's fascinating."

"*I* can't wait to get my hands on it!" If Luca only knew she needed a distraction to keep her hands off him.

CHAPTER EIGHT

EIGHT HOURS LATER, the three of them had eaten dinner and they'd gone back to the living room to work on the puzzle a little longer. It had been a hit and Dino couldn't wait to do more on it before bed.

Luca decided now would be the time to bring up what he'd been dreading most. There was no way to do this but be up-front. He looked at Gabi, who was keyed in to his radar. Then he glanced at his boy's bent head as he was trying to find matching pieces.

"I had some good news today, Dino. Dr. Meuller is back from Africa early, so he's going to meet us at the hospital in the morning and operate on you."

His head reared. "In the morning? I thought it wasn't going to be yet!"

"He had a change in plans. Once it's over, you'll never have to think about it again."

Luca had braced himself for a reaction, and Dino didn't disappoint him. His son almost knocked over the chair running out of the living room. By tacit agreement, Luca and Gabi hurried after him.

Dino had thrown himself on his bed facedown with his sandals still on. Luca removed them and lay down on one side of him. Gabi settled in on his other side.

"We're both here for you, *figlio mio.* You don't have to go through any of this alone."

He started sobbing, the kind that tore your heart out.

"Dino?" Gabi rubbed his back. "Did you know your *mamma* is watching and protecting you? She's been waiting and waiting for you to have the operation so you won't get any more headaches. Think how happy she's going to be when it's over. She'll stop crying and shout *evviva.*"

Luca wasn't sure if she was getting through to him until Dino slowly turned over. "You think she's been crying?"

"Yes, darling. You're her dear, dear son. She's had to wait until Dr. Meuller said it was the right time. I know she's thrilled he came back from Africa sooner so he could make you well sooner. Tomorrow is going to be a happy day for all of us, especially Dr. Meuller."

"Dr. Meuller—" Dino sounded astonished.

"Yes. He has the skill to take your headache away. Isn't that marvelous? Do you have any idea how happy he is every time he takes a child's pain away?"

"Has he done it a lot?"

Gabi had him now. "He's taken away hundreds of headaches," Luca told his son. "Everyone wants him for their doctor, even the people in Africa who don't have enough money to pay him. But he operates for free because he's been blessed with a special gift."

"Just like your *papà* when he won the gold medal in the downhill for our country," Gabi explained. "It brought happiness to millions of people who can't do what he does and wish they could. Not everyone can ski like that and bring joy. Only a few people in the world have that gift. Only a few doctors like Dr. Meuller have *his* gift.

"Only a few people like Gabi have her gift for drawing," Luca interjected. "Think of that butterfly picture above your bed."

"I don't know anyone who can draw like that," Dino said.

"You see? One day you'll find out what *your* gift is, Dino. As soon as your headaches go away, you can start doing all the things you want to do. I bet you want to run with your father in the mornings."

"Yup, and play hockey and soccer!"

"I would love to see you play everything! All you have to do is have that operation in the morning and then we're going to have so much fun!"

Luca held his breath while he waited for Dino's next comment. "Will you two sleep with me tonight?"

"Yes," they both said at once.

Gabi kissed his forehead and got up off the bed. "While you and your dad get ready, I'll run to my room and change into my robe. Then I'll come back and bring a pillow."

"Hurry!"

Luca realized he'd just watched an angel in human form leave the bedroom.

She'd become his rock as well as the woman he wanted in his life forever. Just when he thought he couldn't go on another second, her beautiful, smiling face was there to give him a recharge. He loved her desperately and needed her with every fiber of his being.

* * *

The staff at San Pietro Hospital couldn't have been more wonderful. Gabi followed Dino and his father to the third floor, where he had a large private room. She carried his overnight case, while Luca brought in their overnight bags. She was thankful they'd made it this far without his son breaking down.

The nurse asked Dino to go in the bathroom with her for a minute. When he'd disappeared behind the door, Gabi grasped Luca's hand. "I can only imagine what's going through your mind right now, but I know everything's going to be all right. It has to be."

"You're right." He kissed her swiftly. "What would I do if you weren't here with me?"

"You'd handle it like you've been handling everything all your life. You're a warrior and your son is your greatest success. I've been frightened about the operation, too, but no longer. You know why?

"You brought a son full of confidence into this hospital. He's at the top of the mountain ready to race down the piste after his own medal. You wait and see. In a few hours he'll come out of this with the gold because he has your physical and mental DNA."

Luca drew her into his arms, hugging her so hard she had trouble breathing. He let her go when they heard the bathroom door open.

Dino ran over to them. "What's that?"

Luca grinned at him. "Your hospital gown."

"I have to wear that?"

"I know it's not as exciting as your Star Wars pajamas," Gabi spoke up, "but you only have to keep it on until tomorrow."

Silver-haired Dr. Meuller came in the room and walked right over to Dino with a smile. "Do you remember me?"

"Yes."

"Do you trust me?"

"Yes. This morning we prayed for God to guide your hands."

The doctor looked taken back. "I said the same prayer before I left my house. While my staff takes you to the operating room, your family will stay in the waiting room down the hall. Is that all right?"

Dino nodded. "How long will it take?"

"Maybe two hours. When it's over, I'll tell them how you are, and then they can come visit you in another hour or two after you wake up. How does that sound?"

"Do…other children get scared?"

"I know they do, but I've never seen a boy as brave as you."

"Do doctors get scared?"

One of Dino's gifts was an inquiring mind. Gabi wondered what Dr. Meuller would say. She looked at Luca while she waited.

"Not now that I've said my prayers."

"Me neither."

The doctor squeezed Dino's shoulder and left the room. Luca kissed him. "I'm so proud of you."

"Papà? Are you scared?"

"No. Not at all. We've got Gabi with us. Remember?"

In a minute, two members of the staff walked in. They put Dino on the gurney. *"A presto, mio figlio prediletto."* All the love in the world poured from Luca's broken voice.

Gabi reached for Luca's hand and clung to it while they watched the most precious child in the world being wheeled away to surgery. Alone in the room for a minute, she couldn't help but put her arms around him, wanting to comfort him in the only way she knew how.

He held her tighter until one of the nurses came in with a paper she put on the bed, causing them to pull apart. "Let's go to the cafeteria for a bite to eat," he murmured, "then we'll head for the waiting room."

Gabi wasn't hungry, but they needed energy to keep going. "That's a good idea. I'd like to tell Mamma what's happening."

He brought the paper with them. They walked out to the elevator and rode down to the main floor. Once they reached the cafeteria and went through the line, they found an empty table. While they ate, they both made phone calls. Luca talked with his parents and his secretary at work.

After Gabi hung up, she drank her coffee and read over the instructions that the nurse had brought in to them. Together they discussed the instructions for what to expect post-op. It all depended on how well Dino survived his operation. That was anyone's guess.

She saw the anguish on Luca's face and knew how terrified he was. If only she could relieve him a little. "Dino told me you've had a few operations."

He nodded. "Tonsils and appendix. But the other two were for a broken arm and later a broken hand while I was skiing."

"Your hand?"

"Yes. I skidded on ice down the piste and

bashed into the barricade. My hand took the biggest hit."

"That's terrible. Which arm did you break?"

"My lower left. That time I careened into a tree."

"How fast were you going?"

"Probably a hundred and thirty kilometers an hour. It was a vertical drop."

She groaned. "You were out of your mind."

He smiled. It was the first she'd seen for hours. "You lied to Dino when you said I had a gift. Some would say a downhiller has a death wish."

"Well, I know that's not true of you. I have to tell you I'm very impressed. I've never known an Olympic champion before. One of these days I'd like to watch those hundreds of videos of you in storage. But I won't watch them while Dino is around."

"You'd be wasting your time. If you're ready, shall we go up to the waiting room?"

"Yes." Luca was so restless, but she couldn't blame him. One hour had already passed. Now they had to survive another one before they got any news.

Once upstairs, they counted the minutes. But already it had been two and a half hours since the operation and there was no sign of staff, let alone the doctor. Luca had to be jumping out of his skin.

Sure enough he eventually got up to bring them fresh coffee and some biscotti from the vending machine. By the time three hours had passed, alarm bells had been going off inside her, but she refused to show any fear in front of Luca.

"Something has gone wrong." Luca's pallor had become pronounced. He lowered his head, clasping his hands between his legs, a picture of abject pain. "Dino is probably going to have problems and he'll need health care for the rest of his life. I'm thankful I have the money, but it could mean breaking in someone who will have to live in. That will be hard on Dino at first."

"I don't believe anything's wrong. We just have to hang on a little longer. Remember the sheet said every operation was different. It means the doctor is being careful."

He lifted his head. Lines of anxiety stood out on his handsome face. "Do you have any idea how much your support has meant to me?" His brilliant blue eyes had moistened. "Every time it seemed like I couldn't find the strength to help my son take the next step, *you* were there to point the way along this torturous path. You always turned things around, making it better. My debt to you is beyond my ability to repay."

She put a hand on his arm in response.

Darling, Luca. I don't want repayment. I just want your love.

Another half hour passed. Gabi was ready to run to the nursing station for an update when Dr. Meuller appeared in the waiting room. He was still garbed in his gown and mask.

He pulled it down to reveal a smile on his face. "I didn't intend to keep you in suspense so long, but Dino was a unique case. I wanted to observe him when he first woke up in the event there were any signs of muscle weakness or breathing problems."

She felt Luca's body stiffen.

"There weren't, Signor Berettini. Your son has come out of this operation perfectly normal in every way."

"*La loda spetta a Dio*," Luca whispered.

Gabi grabbed Luca's arm, praising heaven, too. Once again she'd witnessed another miracle.

The doctor smiled at him. "I'm happy to inform you that the surgery was a complete success! Dino will be able to go home on Monday morning and probably won't need anything more than an over-the-counter painkiller for a few days."

Luca shook his head like he was in a daze. "It's really over? I can't believe it."

The older man patted his shoulder. "There'll be no more headaches. What's important now is that Dino recovers now and after the new year he can go back to school and his activities."

"So he doesn't have to lie low for months and months?" Luca sounded incredulous. Gabi could see he was still in shock over the news.

"No, no. No more limitations. I'll ask you to bring him in after the new year for a checkup. If you have any questions, call me. You can go back to his room now. They'll be wheeling him in shortly. He's awake and doing remarkably well."

Tears streamed down Gabi's face. "There are no words to thank you, Doctor."

"I got my thanks when Dino woke up and said, 'When are you going to do the operation, Dr. Meuller?'"

Luca burst into the happiest laughter she'd

ever heard in her life before he crushed Gabi against him. They both felt reborn. The doctor waved to them before leaving the waiting room.

"He's going to be fine now, Gabi!" Luca cried, rocking her for a long time before he grabbed her hand. They hurried through the hallway to Dino's room. Since he still hadn't come in yet, they both got on their phones to send out the joyous news that the operation had been a total success.

Gabi called her mother, then Edda. The older woman broke down in tears. She said she would tell the whole building. As they hung up, there was an orderly at the door and here came Dino on the gurney with part of his head wrapped.

"Papà. I'm all well!"

"I know. Dr. Meuller told us."

How could he sound this wonderful after what he'd been through? Gabi couldn't get over it.

Once Dino was helped into the bed, Gabi watched Luca embrace his son and saw his shoulders heave.

"Why are you crying, Papà?"

"I only cry when I'm happy."

"You must be really happy! I bet Mamma is really crying hard, too."

"I know she is."

"So is Dr. Meuller. So am I!" Gabi exclaimed. She hurried over to his other side, careful not to disturb the IV drip, and kissed his forehead.

Then Dino's grandparents came in the room. While Luca talked with his son, this was Gabi's first chance to meet his father. She moved away from the bed toward them.

The physical resemblance between the two men was extraordinary, both in coloring and build. They were a beautiful family. Giustina made the introductions before hurrying over to Dino.

"Signora Parisi?" his father said. "Our family is in your debt for making these last few weeks more bearable for little Dino. My wife told me about the letter he printed. I understand he really loves that television program. Now I know why."

"Thank you, Signor Berettini."

"Please tell Signora Romano we're grateful for her foundation. She does a great service for children. I'm sure you've been missed and she's anxious to have you back."

On that note he nodded to the other couple that had just walked in the room with another gift. "Tomaso and Maria? Come over here and meet one of the employees from the Start with a Wish foundation."

Gabi recognized the dark-haired couple from the photos. "I'm so pleased to meet you. Dino has talked about you a lot while we've put puzzles and building blocks together."

Tomaso smiled. "He says you like to eat chocolate-covered insects."

That made her laugh. "Then don't tell him the truth. Please. He loves chocolate *bocci* balls."

"We would have brought him some but know they're not good for him. They were Catarina's favorite candy, too. We brought him a game instead."

"He loves games."

"You've made a real hit with him, indulging him as you have," Maria said. "So many gifts we've heard about when we talk to him on the phone. Even a framed drawing from you hanging over his bed. Do you visit every child who writes to you?"

"No. There are different departments in place to make a child's wish come true. I work with a group of women who read the letters when they first come in. We screen them before turning them over to Edda Romano, who heads the program. She determines what will happen next. But Dino was a special case.

"Edda wanted someone from the foundation to take him a gift in person. She asked me to take him a building blocks game since she couldn't grant him the wish he really wanted."

"What was that?"

"He wanted his mother to be there for the operation."

"Of course he did." Maria put a hand to her throat and tears came to her eyes.

"Everyone at the foundation had the same reaction to his letter as you, Signora Guardino. A mother is irreplaceable."

Tomaso nodded. "There was no one like Catarina. We loved her so much. She was the perfect mother and wife. There'll never be anyone like her. Thank heaven Dino has come through this to help Luca go on living. Now he can really dig into his work, eh, Fabrizo?"

"Amen to that," Luca's father added and focused his gaze on Gabi. "Since we won't be seeing you again, Signora Parisi, we thank you for your time."

He didn't expect to see her again? How odd that sounded.

While she stood there trying to understand him, everyone clustered around Dino. Gabi feared it was too much excitement for him, and wondered why a nurse hadn't come in yet. But she also recognized that she'd been in protective mode around him since knowing him and needed to stop worrying. Luca hadn't seemed to notice, so why should she be concerned?

She watched Catarina's aunt and uncle. Dino was like a grandchild to them. They were all very close-knit, especially after such a tragedy. But Luca's father had given off a different aura to her.

Dino acted thrilled to see everyone and kept talking. Gabi had been so used to him seeking her out, she felt…she didn't know exactly how or what she felt… Oh, yes, she did. Whom was she kidding? She felt like an outsider.

That's what she was, a woman from the foundation who'd brought him a gift in response to his letter. Deep down she felt Luca's father resented her for some reason. She didn't want to be unkind about him, but there was no mistaking a certain tension he'd given off just now.

While they were all talking, she picked up that they were staying at a hotel in town. They would be coming over to the hospital for the next few days to keep Dino company until he went home.

The only thing she could see to do was be with her mom for the night. That way Luca would be free to visit with everyone for as long as he wanted and spend private time with his son. This would be the perfect time to bow out.

She slipped out of the room and walked around the corner to use the restroom and freshen up. When she came back out with the intention of telling Luca her plan, she rounded the corner again and saw him in the corridor with his father. Their backs were turned toward her. She had the impression they were arguing. All she heard was, "Now that Dino is better, you have to marry Giselle, do you hear me?"

CHAPTER NINE

MARRY GISELLE? Who was she?

Gabi felt like she'd been stabbed and hurried back to the restroom in agony. Luca had never mentioned that woman to her. But apparently he'd been involved with her before Gabi had come on the scene because Signor Berettini knew all about her. What on earth did any of it mean?

His remarks to Gabi no longer puzzled her. It made sense that he thought he'd seen the last of her. The older man would be shocked if he knew she and Luca had kissed passionately, let alone that Dino had asked her to be his *mamma.*

Gabi sank down on the couch and called her mother again. The moment she heard her voice, she broke down.

"Darling—whatever is wrong? This should be the happiest night of your life!"

"For a little while it was."

"You said Dino's going to be fine."

"He is, and he won't have to go through a long recovery period. I guess I thought I might be needed for a lot longer, but that isn't the case."

"I see."

"The doctor wants him in school after the new year. He's in amazing health now. All the trauma is over."

"Isn't that wonderful!"

"It is."

"But it means your life is going to get back to normal, too."

Her mother understood. "Yes. Tonight as I watched him laughing and talking with his family, I realized Dino has faced his fear and overcome it. He doesn't need me any longer."

"Darling—you're always going to be his friend."

"I know, but it won't be the same. All I've done is tell you my problems since I married Santos. It's not fair to you. I'm going to hang up now. In a little while I'll get a taxi and come home for the night. See you soon."

After hanging up, she left the restroom. When she looked around the corner, Luca was still there, but he was alone. He walked toward her, his expression glowing with happiness.

Already a transformation had taken place. Those deep grief lines on his unforgettably handsome face were receding. There was a new light in his eyes she'd never seen before.

"I've been waiting for you." No mention of his father.

"Sorry I was so long. I called my mother to tell her about Dino and let her know I'll be home in a little while."

What had she said about those receding tension lines on his face? They came back with a vengeance. "I couldn't have heard you right. You promised Dino you'd stay here with him."

"I'll be back first thing in the morning. Your family is here tonight to be with him."

Luca's black brows met in a frown. "They'll be leaving soon to go to their hotel. Dino expects you and me to be here until we all go home on Monday. He's just had surgery. I don't want him upset by anything. If he found out you weren't here, I don't even want to think about it."

"Luca—you don't have to be afraid for him anymore. He knows he's fine. Everything is different now."

"The hell it is." For the first time since she'd known him, his response gave her a glimpse of the tough CEO he could be when necessary. "The operation has changed nothing for him where his feelings for you are concerned. You don't honestly think this has been some kind of an act for him—"

"No. Of course not, but given time—"

"Given time he'll what?" Luca cut her off. "Now that the danger is over, you imagine he'll just switch back to the way he was before you came into his life? What's happened to you since Dr. Meuller gave us the incredible news?"

Oh, Luca. If only she dared tell him what she'd overheard. Gabi had no idea what it had all meant, but she could see that tonight was not the time to have this discussion.

"I just didn't want to be in the way."

His expression looked like thunder. "What are you talking about? If Dino had his way, he wouldn't have anyone else around."

"That's not true."

"Whom are you trying to convince? The families will be leaving any minute now, and I've ordered cots to be brought in for both of us."

"Please don't be upset, Luca. I never meant to cause you this much concern."

His chest rose and fell visibly. "As long as there's no more talk of you going anywhere, I can handle anything. This is a night for celebration."

She nodded. So be it for now. Gabi would have to text her mother that plans had changed once again. "It is! Now you can be happy. All our prayers have been answered."

His fierce gaze played over her, as if he were still having trouble settling down after she'd said she was leaving. "Dino's expecting us to come back in the room." He really was upset. She'd never seen Luca this formidable before. "Gabi—"

She could hardly breathe for the intense way he was looking at her. "What is it?"

His compelling mouth tightened. "Nothing. Are you ready?"

"Of course."

They walked back to the room together. It killed her to think that she'd upset him on this night of all nights. Everyone was still there. Luca's father watched them come inside. After what she'd overheard, it was hard to pretend everything was fine, that she wasn't in pain.

Maria kissed Dino, who was finally winding down. He'd closed his eyes. Gabi loved him so much she could hardly stand it.

"I think we should go, Tomaso." Dino's grandmother followed suit. Everyone hugged and smiled at Gabi. "We'll see you in the morning."

Signor Berettini left last. He nodded to Gabi and took his son aside to talk to him in private for a moment as they walked toward the door. Gabi turned away from them and walked over to the side of the bed. To her surprise Dino's eyelids fluttered open.

"Are you going to stay with me tonight?"

Guilt washed over her that she'd contemplated leaving him tonight. Whatever was going on in Luca's personal life, she'd made a commitment to this boy. "As if I'd be anywhere else."

"Good. *Ti amo*, Gabi."

"*Ti amo*, darling. Sweet dreams." She kissed his cheek before he fell asleep.

Out of the corner of her eye she saw Luca's father leave. The three of them were finally alone. A second later an employee from housekeeping wheeled in two cots.

She watched as Luca set them up and placed

them side by side at the end of the bed. After sleeping on either side of Dino last night, the dynamics of the situation weren't anything new, but the stakes had changed because with one operation Dino had been cured.

"He looks so peaceful," she remarked.

Luca walked over and whispered, "I'd like to keep him that way."

"You haven't forgiven me yet, have you?"

She heard a deep sigh escape. "There's nothing to forgive. I'm afraid I've lived in fear so long, I can't quite believe the nightmare is over. If anything, I need to beg your forgiveness. The support from family has been vital, but you and I have been a team. The thought of that changing tonight threw me."

It threw me, too, Luca.

But he didn't know what she'd heard his father say out in the hall.

Gabi stood by as an attractive nurse came in to check Dino's drip and make notations on the computer. She smiled at Luca. Gabi recognized that look. She bet the nurse had never seen a more gorgeous man in her life. "Your son is doing great. I'll be in later."

After she left, Gabi removed her shoes and

lay down on one of the cots. "The news just keeps getting better and better."

He leaned over and brushed his lips against hers. "Thank heaven. I don't know about you, but I'm suddenly exhausted."

"I honestly don't know how you've survived these last two years. I'm so happy it's over for you and Dino."

She turned on her side to watch as he removed his shoes and stretched out on his cot. His long, rock-hard body was too big. He'd never be able to sleep on it. She'd never get to sleep while she could still feel his mouth on hers.

"Incredible to believe he's fine now." Luca put his hands behind his head. "But we wouldn't have made it these last few weeks without you," he said in a quiet tone. "I'll never forget the moment this beautiful blonde woman walked into the foundation reception room.

"When you told Dino you weren't mad at him, he ran to you as if you were the most important person in his universe. I'll never forget it because I hadn't seen that kind of emotion since he lost his mother."

"Meeting Dino was a life-changing moment for me, too, Luca. When I was first married, I wanted a baby so badly. My parents could only have one child, and I always wanted brothers and sisters. So I hoped to have a big family, maybe three or four children.

"But as you know, that dream was dashed. Then I met Dino, the epitome of my idea of the perfect boy. I thought, how could any parent be so lucky to have such a cute, fun-loving, charming son like him. To realize he'd lost his mother just killed me.

"I know I've gone overboard with him, but I haven't been able to help myself. When he asked me if I liked Paolo more than I liked him, I wanted to shout, 'Can't you tell? Can't you see I'm crazy about you?'"

"I believe it was meant to be, Gabi," he said in a smoky voice. "Last night you were able to calm Dino's fears in a way I never could. I was too close to it. He actually slept until we woke him up to drive him here."

"The cute thing was so good and brave. Just think, tomorrow he wakes up to a brand-new world where everything and anything is possible. Go to sleep now, Luca. No one deserves it more than you do. *Buona notte.*"

She turned away from him and closed her eyes. Gabi needed to get undressed, take a shower, wash her hair and sob her heart out. But she couldn't do any of it. For the next little while she lay there reliving every second of her life since she'd first met Dino and his father.

You goose, Gabi. You've been living in a fantasy world.

She'd thought she'd learned her lesson after getting married to the wrong man. There'd been warning signs all over the place, but she'd refused to pick up on them because it had been so wonderful to be in love like her friends. Too late she realized it hadn't been love everlasting or anything close to it.

Now that she'd met the most marvelous, incredible man in existence and knew she would never love like this again, his father had sent out another warning sign. Tonight in this hospital room she'd seen and heard it loud and clear.

Saturday and Sunday turned out to be constantly busy days helping Dino get back to some kind of normal. He had to take walks and get another X-ray. Luca and Gabi kept him entertained between the routine tests, checks from Dr. Meuller and short visits by the family.

Luca had warned his father to stay off the

subject of Giselle or he wasn't welcome at the hospital. For once his father left him alone about it, but he knew it wouldn't be over after they got home.

When Monday morning rolled around, he felt like they'd all been let out of prison. While the nurse pushed Dino's wheelchair out to the hospital loading area with Gabi at his side, Luca brought the car around. Dr. Meuller had unwrapped the roll of gauze from Dino's head and replaced it with a small patch behind his ear that wasn't noticeable.

A fresh snowstorm had blanketed the town. With all the Christmas decorations along the streets, there was a festive nature in the air. Dino loved being out in it. They all loved it. The second Dino climbed in the backseat, he bounced for joy.

"*Evviva!* I'm going home!" Luca no longer had to worry that his son was moving around too much. "Can we stop and get a *fondente gelato* with *panna* on the way?"

Gabi rolled her eyes at Luca. "That sounds good to me, too. I want the same thing, but with *zabaglione*."

He flashed her a smile that curled her toes. "You remembered."

"That was a very special day."

Once they'd found a *gelateria*, they enjoyed their treats and took off for Maniago. "Do I have to go to bed when I get home?"

"Only if you feel like lying down."

"When do you have to go to work, Papà?"

Luca chuckled. "After Christmas, but I'll put in a few hours at the office here and there."

"What about you, Gabi?"

"I'm still on vacation," she spoke up, relieving Luca's mind.

His car ate up the miles. Gabi started a game and got them counting how many blue cars they saw, then they switched to black cars. It kept his son busy because she knew how to make everything exciting.

When the three of them ran out of cars to count, it seemed to be the best time for the announcement. If Luca didn't make it, his son was going to drive them all crazy before they reached Maniago.

"*Ehi, figlio mio?* I thought we'd stop and pick up a friend for you to play with on our way home."

"What? A friend—Paolo's my friend, but he's at school."

"You can always use another one at home."

Four months ago Luca had planned on getting Dino a dog once his operation was over. He'd been in touch with the owner of a litter of twelve-week-old pups. Depending on how successful the operation was, he'd been planning to spring the good news on Dino later in the week. But necessity dictated that today had to be the day.

Gabi shot him a glance. He hadn't told her his plan, but with that razor-sharp brain of hers, she'd probably figured it out.

"I don't want to play with anyone else. Can't we just go home, Papà?"

"I think you'll change your mind when you meet her."

"Her—?"

Gentle laughter escaped Gabi's lips.

"Or him. Tell you what. I'll let you decide after we get to this lady's house."

"Where is it?"

"Here in Maniago, not far from our villa. We're almost there."

Luca shared another glance with Gabi, who was smiling. He felt her excitement as he followed the curving road and drove into an estate where the snow was a little deeper. After winding around to the rear entrance, he came to a stop and turned off the engine.

"Shall we get out?"

On cue an older woman came out the door in slacks and an apron.

"Signora Borelli? Please meet my son, Dino, and our friend Signora Parisi."

His son looked bewildered.

"I understand you just got out of the hospital, Dino. Would you like to come in on my back porch for a minute?"

Dino walked over to grasp Luca's hand before they walked through the snow and went inside. There they discovered half a dozen black-and-white border collie puppies running around their mother.

"Oh, Dino—" Gabi cried in delight as the puppies scrambled over to them. "Aren't these dogs adorable!" She reached down to pick up one of them and carefully handed it Dino, who looked so happy, Luca thought he was going to cry. The dog squirmed and licked his son, who couldn't stop giggling.

"We have four males and two females."

A pair of blue eyes looked up at Luca. "Can I have a boy dog?"

The woman lifted the dog out of his arms

and picked up another one. "Now you can pick out one of the boys. They're twelve weeks old, close to being trained, have had their shots and are ready to go home."

Dino stared at Luca. "I don't know which one to pick."

"I have an idea," Gabi said. "Why don't you play with all of them and see which one seems to appeal to you the most. Maybe one of them will want to go home with you and let you know."

Luca's heart melted while he watched his son have the time of his life calling to each pup and running around with them. He wasn't the only one having a marvelous time. Gabi's eyes shone with a joy she couldn't hide because he knew she was a dog lover and had owned one. These pups were irresistible.

After a few minutes it became apparent his son couldn't make up his mind. He kept holding one, then another one. "I wish we could take them all home, Papà."

That produced laughter from everyone.

Gabi knelt down by him. "Their faces are all different."

"I know. Which one do you like?"

"It's hard to choose. I guess I kind of like

the one where the black covers up one eye, like a mask. Once when I worked at a pet store, I watched people pick out their favorite dog or cat. No one wanted this one little beagle who was small and whiny. But I loved him and the owner let me take him home."

"You named him Tex, huh?"

"I did. I guess you have to decide which dog touches your heart."

"The one with the mask looks the funniest. Do you think people would laugh at him?"

"Probably, but he won't know why. He doesn't look in a mirror. He thinks he's just like his brothers and sisters."

"Yeah."

Even Signora Borelli laughed at Gabi's comment.

"Why don't you pick up each dog again and have a talk with him. Maybe then you'll be able to make up your mind."

Gabi could get Luca's son to do anything. He watched him catch each one and walk over in a corner to have a private conversation between licks. When he'd finished, he came over to Luca. "I can't decide."

"Then we'll come back tomorrow and take another look."

"But what if one of them is gone?"

"That's a possibility," Gabi remarked. "They're all so darling."

While they stood there, the puppy Luca now thought of as the masked puppy kept jumping around Dino.

"Do you know what I think?" They all looked at the owner. "That dog has picked you, Dino. He won't leave you alone."

"I know. He keeps running around me. I think he likes me."

"I know he does. They choose the master they want."

"They do?"

The owner nodded. "I see it happen over and over again. Someone comes in, and one of the litter chooses them. Nature is an amazing thing."

A huge smile broke out on Dino's face. He picked up the pup and was rewarded with half a dozen licks. He broke down laughing and looked at him. "How come he loves me so much?"

Luca glanced at Gabi, who was beaming. "That's just how it happens, with animals and people. No one can explain love at first sight, but it's a fact of life."

Do you hear me, Gabi?

It was love at first sight with them, but they'd both had to get past their own painful pasts to recognize it for what it was.

"Can we take him home now?"

"What do you think?"

"I have a dog crate you can buy," the owner said.

In a few minutes the transaction had been made and they left for the villa. The dog sat in the crate on the backseat next to Dino, who was entranced. Luca would set up a box to keep in the family room until the dog was fully trained.

After they got home, he carried the crate into the family room and everyone, including the staff, gathered round. They could see Dino was in great shape and hugged him.

"Guess what? I got a dog!" Everyone laughed.

Luca said, "After lunch I'll run to the pet shop and get the things we need. Then we'll let him out."

Ines stood there with her hands on her hips. "What's his name?"

"Nero," Dino announced. "He has a black eye. I love him!"

Luca patted his shoulder. "That's a good

name for him, just like the emperor in your Coliseum puzzle. Now why don't you wash your hands and we'll eat the special pizza lunch Pia has prepared for you."

"Yum. *Grazie*, Pia. They didn't give me pizza in the hospital."

"I shouldn't think so."

The dog whimpered as they started to leave the room. "Don't cry, Nero. I'll be right back."

The dog wouldn't take the place of Gabi, but Dino would be so busy taking care of him, he wouldn't miss her so horribly when she did have to go back to work. However, Luca knew that would only be for a very short period while he made future plans for the three of them.

Before long Nero had a collar, a leash, puppy dog food and two bowls for meat and water. They kept the dog on the leash to take him outside, and to keep him near Dino in case the door was open to the other rooms. The training would take time, but with luck Nero would be fully trained in sixteen weeks.

A boy and his dog.

Gabi watched him run around the house with Nero getting in the way, running ahead and then behind him. Dino was free to do whatever he wanted. She loved Luca for thinking of this gift for him. Nothing could be more perfect than to start off his whole new life with a constant companion.

Gabi was so happy for him she felt like she could burst, but nothing could erase the pain when she remembered what she'd heard Luca's father say to him in private.

By late afternoon Luca insisted Dino stop for a while and take a nap on his bed. He'd had a huge day. They went upstairs and Luca carried the crate.

"Gabi? How soon do you have to leave?"

"Day after tomorrow. Since there's more snow forecast, I'll have to get up really early so I won't be too late for work. But you know I'll be back."

"But you're going to sleep here tonight and tomorrow night?"

"Yes."

"Will you and Papà take me when I go back to school?"

Pain, pain. "I'm sure I will."

"Will you sleep with me?"

"No, Dino," Luca spoke for her. "She has to stay in her own bed. We all do because we need a good night's sleep. But she'll be down the hall. And don't forget—Nero will be next to your bed in his crate like he is right now. You can talk to him and make him feel better because he'll be missing his mother and will cry during the night."

"He will?"

"Yes. All he's ever known are his mom and his brothers and sisters. You're going to be his new family."

"Don't worry. I'll take care of him."

The love in Dino's voice finished Gabi off. She excused herself to go to the guest bedroom. This had been a day like no other. She'd been storing up memories because starting day after tomorrow she needed to make new ones that had nothing to do with Dino or Luca.

Luisa had texted her, wondering if they could go to dinner and a movie soon. She texted her back and made a date for Friday after work. Then she got in the shower and washed her hair. After drying it, she slipped on a blouse and skirt. Before she went downstairs, she lay down on top of the bed just to close her eyes for a minute.

When she heard Luca call to her, at first she

thought she was dreaming until he said her name again. "Gabi?"

She sat up. How long had she been sleeping? It was dark outside. "Luca?"

"We need to talk. Can I come in?"

"Please do. Is Dino all right?"

"I gave him a painkiller. Now he's out like a light and will probably stay that way until morning. I've already taken Nero out again."

"Have you had any rest yet?" He had to be utterly exhausted.

"Don't worry about me." Her door was still open, so they could hear Dino if he called out.

Luca moved over to the bed and stretched out on it next to her. "I need to hold you for a little while." In the next breath he pulled her into his arms and buried his face in her hair.

Gabi couldn't believe this was happening. The mention of another woman in his life had been eating away at her emotions, but this was what she'd been wanting for so long, she could deny him nothing.

Euphoric that she had the freedom to touch and feel him, she pushed her fears aside and gave in to her desires. They came together in an explosion of need that rocked her world.

"You don't know what meeting you has done

to me." He kissed every centimeter of her face and throat. "I could eat you alive. Don't ask me to stop because I can't, *bellissima*."

"I don't want you to stop. Surely you know that by now. Why else do I keep finding excuses to stay?"

"I love you, Gabriella Russo. I'm so in love with you, I can't think about anything else. Don't say it's too soon, or that we barely know each other. None of that matters because we know how we feel."

So how did he feel about the woman named Giselle? What was the truth of that situation? She could ask him but didn't want Luca to think that she'd been eavesdropping earlier.

"I knew I wanted you the moment I saw you at the foundation. If you can deny that you didn't feel the same way, then you're lying to yourself and to me."

"I'm not denying anything, Luca. Over the last few weeks I've learned to love you more than life itself. You know I have. In truth I didn't think it possible to love any man like I do you. I didn't know a man like you existed, but here you are. And you're the father to the most perfect boy in the world. Half the time I feel I must be dreaming."

"Then we're both in the same dream. Love me, Gabi," he cried, before he started devouring her.

Being in his arms like this, being swept away by his kisses that grew longer and deeper had her spinning out of control. She could hold nothing back. Their desire for each other was reaching flashpoint. He rolled her on top of him, trapping her legs. She gasped as he molded her to his hard, male body. This kind of rapture was indescribable.

"*Ti amo*," she cried, witless and breathless.

But in the next breath she heard whimpering sounds at the side of the bed that caused her to lift her head.

"Good grief. It's Nero," Luca muttered.

Before she had the presence of mind to move off him, the overhead light went on.

There stood Dino. "Papà! Are you and Gabi making a baby?"

Caught like rats in a trap as they old saying went. Another minute and they wouldn't have been wearing their clothes. She was on the verge of hysteria.

Luca rolled her over and got up from the bed. "What do you know about making babies?" Calm and collected. That was the man she adored.

"Paolo told me."

"That Paolo has a lot to answer for." He picked up the puppy. "How come you let Nero out of his crate?"

"He was whining and it woke me up. I thought I'd put him up on the bed, but he ran away from me."

"Now you know why you have to keep him on a leash."

"I'm sorry."

"That's okay. This is how you learn. Come on. We'll go downstairs and take him outside. Are you hungry?"

"No. I just want some water."

"Are you going to come, too, Gabi?"

"Let's leave her alone until she's ready."

"I'll be downstairs in a minute, Dino."

"Are you going to have a baby?"

"We'll let you know when we know."

She couldn't believe Luca had just said that and shut her eyes tightly, hardly daring to breathe. Gabi ran in the bathroom to fix her makeup and brush her hair. After straightening her clothes, she hurried downstairs. The grandfather clock chimed 9:30 p.m. She assumed the staff had gone to bed in the other wing of the villa.

Gabi went to the kitchen to wait for them. Pretty soon the two of them came in. "Where's Nero?"

"Papà put him in the crate in the family room for the rest of the night."

"I think that's a good idea. It's time for everyone to get to bed."

Dino pulled a bottle of water from the fridge. He hurried over to her and gave her a hug. "I know you said you'd stay until the day after tomorrow, but I wish you didn't have to go."

"I promise I'll be back. Have I ever broken one?"

"No."

"All right then. *Buona notte*, Dino."

He acted like he wanted to say more, but Luca gave him a look and that was enough to silence him. "I'll meet you in the living room," Luca mouthed on the way out of the kitchen.

A few minutes ago they'd been interrupted before a huge mistake had been made. Now Luca wanted to talk about it. She trembled like a leaf while she curled up on one end of the couch waiting for him.

At ten after ten Luca entered the living room and found Gabi right where he wanted her. He reached for her and pulled her onto his lap. "How about that son of mine?" he said against her lips. "I'm sorry I left your bedroom door open so the dog could get in."

She took a quick breath. "I'm glad you did. It woke me up to reality."

"The only reality is that I'm in love with you and want to marry you right away. After tonight it's obvious we need to be man and wife as soon as possible."

He tried to prolong their kiss, but she had to get away from him. Calling on every shred of self-discipline, Gabi slid off his lap so she could stand.

"We can't. *You* can't."

"What's to stop us?"

"For one thing, common sense."

Luca looked up at her in amazement. "We're both mature adults who've experienced marriage before. We know what we feel now. I want you to be my wife. I want to give you children we'll raise together with Dino. With you at my side, I see the chance for a lifetime of happiness for all of us. I know you do, too."

"I thought I did until the day Dino was operated on."

He got to his feet. His jaw had hardened. "What do you mean?"

She shook her head. "I hadn't intended to say anything, but at this point I can't keep this from you any longer."

"I'm afraid you've lost me."

Gabi kneaded her hands. "When your father entered the room and we were introduced, he thanked me for coming in response to Dino's letter. Later, when everyone was leaving he said something that gave me pause."

Luca's mouth had become a straight line of what she could only interpret as anger. "Tell me exactly," he whipped out.

She swallowed hard. "Tomaso had just made the comment that now that Dino was going to be fine, you could get back to work full-time. He smiled at your father when he said it. Your father in turn looked me straight in the eyes and said, 'Since we won't be seeing you again, Signora Parisi, we thank you for your time.'"

A harsh epithet escaped Luca's lips. "How dare he speak to you like that—as if you were a servant no longer needed. It's so like him," his voice grated. "No wonder you disappeared from the room for so long." He reached out to grip her shoulders. "I swear I'll never let him get near you again. He'll have nothing to do with us or our plans."

She eased away from him. "From the beginning I've sensed you and your father had some kind of a problem. I wondered if that was the reason you didn't want to be the CEO in the first place, but I never wanted to ask."

"I should have explained about him before now, but I've been so worried about Dino, I put it off. Please don't worry about him."

"I can't help it. You haven't heard everything yet."

His dark brows furrowed. "What more is there?"

"Luca—you didn't hear the conversation when everyone had assembled in Dino's room. Catarina's aunt and uncle, along with your father, painted a picture of life with your wife I'll never forget."

Lines marred his handsome features. He put his hands on his hips. "What picture?"

"Don't pretend you don't know what I mean."

"*What picture?*" he ground out.

Gabi moistened her lips nervously. "You and Catarina had the perfect marriage."

"No," he protested. "We had a good marriage despite a lot of differences between us. Like all marriages, it had its ups and downs. Dino was the best part of it. So it's already started," he muttered.

"What do you mean?"

"My father knows something monumental has gone on between you and me. He sensed it when Dino didn't want them to come over for a visit that day. The truth is, he's had a woman picked out for me since I was twenty years old and had almost finished college."

"You're talking about Giselle."

His head reared. "How did you hear about her?"

She took a deep breath. "After I came out of the restroom, I saw you and your father talking in the hall and overheard part of your conversation."

Those blue eyes had narrowed to slits. "What part?"

"He said you had to marry Giselle."

Luca paced the floor before coming to a stop. "Her name is Giselle Fournier. She's the daughter from a wealthy French industrialist family that made their money in plastics. Her father is my father's best friend. I was never interested in her, never could be. She's still available. My father is hopeful I'll marry her to seal the family fortunes."

"You're kidding—"

"He hopes you'll go back to Padova where you came from. That's why he said what he did at the hospital." Luca groaned. "You have no idea what depths my father will sink to in order to get his own way."

"I can't comprehend it. My father was so kind."

"You were lucky. From the time I was born, I'm afraid mine had an agenda where I was concerned. But when he tried to coerce me into marriage, I rebelled openly against him.

"After getting my business degree, I joined the ski team without his knowledge, and there wasn't anything he could do about it. From the age of twenty-one to twenty-five, I lived the life of a racer with my ski buddies all over Europe, even trained in the US and South America. As you pointed out, he didn't even come to watch me race for the gold medal.

"He threatened to cut me off, but I financed myself with racing money and endorsements so he didn't have to pay for anything."

"That's a horror story."

"In a way, it was. About that time, he had a heart attack and blamed me."

"Oh, no—"

"It wasn't a bad one. The doctor said to look at it as a warning. Wouldn't you know the chairman of the board of the company asked me to come in and take over my father's position while he recovered? I saw it as a ploy on my father's part to get me under his thumb. I refused.

"But Mamma begged me to reconsider for her sake. I adore her and since she'd always supported me in everything I did, I knew she was relying on me so I joined the company in an official capacity. Soon after that, I met Catarina and married her. This took my father by complete surprise. *I* was surprised it didn't bring on another heart attack."

He was feeding her so much information, Gabi couldn't believe it. She had so many questions. "Where were you married?"

"In Venice at her family church. I'll show you pictures."

"Did your father attend?"

"No. He pretended that he couldn't come because of his heart condition. Everyone who knew the truth was scandalized by his behavior, but I had my mother, plus lots of ski friends and members of the board who supported us."

"How hard all that must have been for you."

"He's always been a hard man and his own worst enemy. I knew he'd been waiting for me to cave in and get together with Giselle. My marriage to Catarina infuriated him, particularly because the Guardino family had no money or influence. It inflamed him more when I offered Tomaso a better position in the company because I knew it would make Catarina happy."

Gabi was absolutely stunned over what she was hearing now.

"The most important thing you need to know is that my father only tolerated Dino after he was born. My son doesn't know the reason, but he's aware he doesn't have a loving grandfather."

"That I *can't* believe, not when he's the dearest boy on earth."

"Be thankful you haven't ever known anyone like him. After Catarina was killed, he started in again talking about a marriage to Giselle."

"There's something wrong with him."

"Agreed. Mamma finally admitted something to me recently that I'd never known. She said that he and Giselle's father had a business together after the war years, but they couldn't sustain it between their two countries. So they made a pact to get their two children together. My father swore her to secrecy, but she wanted me to know the truth when she could see I would never bend to my father's will."

Gabi folded her arms to her waist. "It sounds like the story of two kings arranging affairs of state and treating their own children like chattel."

Luca smiled without mirth. "Exactly. He missed his calling as one. Now he's worried about *you*, with good reason."

Gabi averted her eyes. "This puts a different complexion on everything."

"I had no idea you'd been holding all of this in since the hospital."

She buried her face in her hands, incredulous over what she'd heard.

"The rest of the family can see how I feel about you, and I know for a fact they approve. You're the best thing that has happened to Dino and me since the avalanche, and they know it. They love him."

"Who wouldn't—?" she said.

"Gabi—" He put his arms around her neck. "You and I were meant to be together. I know it in my DNA. So do you. I don't care how long we've known each other. I want to marry you.

"My *mamma* considers you an angel from heaven. The staff never want you to leave the villa, and Nero came straight to your room. They say a dog follows a gentle heart."

"Luca—" she whispered in tears.

"So I'm not letting you out of my arms until you say yes, that you'll marry me."

She cradled his face in her hands. "You make it sound so simple, so easy."

"Why isn't it? I'll come to Padova. We'll call the priest and make arrangements for the wedding. I want to marry you right away. My father might try to cause more trouble, but he'll be powerless to get away with anything."

Gabi shook her head. "You don't know what you're saying! You haven't even met my mother yet, or my friends. I've been divorced, and it was ugly. I have a position with Edda, who depends on all of us at the foundation."

"She's a tycoon, Gabi, a woman who understands life. When you tell her we're going to be married, do you honestly think she would stand in your way?"

"No," she admitted. "Of course not."

"Then what are you afraid of? Forget my father."

"Y-you wouldn't understand," her voice faltered.

"Try me."

She eased away from him. "You're not thinking clearly right now. Too much has been going on to confuse the issue for both of us. Given time you'll—"

"I'll what?" he cut her off. "There's no other woman for me."

She flinched.

"Have you looked at yourself in the mirror lately? Have you noticed every man on the street practically having an accident as you walk by because they're so taken by your beauty? How about Paolo? Do you remember the excitement on his face when he asked if you'd be at the villa again and Dino said yes?

"Have you seen into my son's eyes and noticed anything but genuine love? Have you forgotten you're the reason he found the courage to have the operation? Talk about the perfect woman..."

Gabi could hear what he was saying. He believed what he was saying. *She* wanted to believe it. But how long would his feelings for her last?

"Tell me what's wrong, Gabi!"

She took a deep breath. "I thought Santos would love me forever. He said and did all the right things and swept naive little me off my feet. I was flattered that the bank manager who had a solid position had fallen for me. When I conceived so fast, I was in heaven.

"But then I miscarried and when I needed to talk about it, Santos always seemed to be preoccupied or working late. He didn't comfort me. It was a terrible time for me. It wasn't long before my friend at the bank told me about his long-term affair with another woman. I thought it was true that a man couldn't be satisfied with one woman.

"I'd married forever, or so I'd thought. If I marry you, I want it to be forever, but what if something happens and your feelings change for me? It terrifies me to think of being married to you, then lose you. Luca—I can't answer you right now, but I promise I'll go home and think about it."

"For how long?" he demanded. Just then he

sounded like Dino. They were both so much alike that way. Once their minds were made up, they acted swiftly with no regrets.

"Trust me. Not long. Now I need to get to bed. Please don't follow me. Morning will be here before we know it and we'll be busy helping Dino learn how to take care of his new dog."

Gabi raced out of the living room and up the stairs. She cried herself to sleep, which was the last thing she should be doing. Luca wanted to marry her. Dino had survived his operation and had been given a clean bill of health. There shouldn't be a dark cloud in her sky. But Santos's betrayal after losing their baby had come back to haunt her.

Morning came when Dino brought Nero to her bedroom door on a leash. His barking woke her up. She lifted her head. "Come on in!"

"He's already minding me, Gabi!"

She was amazed that Dino acted as if he hadn't undergone brain surgery. "That doesn't surprise me." He'd dressed in jeans and a T-shirt and loved his dog so much it did her heart good.

Gabi hurried in the bathroom to get dressed. Then they went downstairs to the kitchen, where Pia had fixed breakfast. Luca walked in a minute later looking rugged and gorgeous in jeans and a navy crew neck sweater. He hadn't shaved yet, making him more attractive than ever. He hunkered down in front of Nero and scratched his head.

"Are you being a good dog?"

"He's the best, Papà!"

"While you eat, I'll take him outside, then we'll settle down and work on that puzzle. Tomaso phoned a minute ago. They stayed at your grandparents' last night. He and Maria will be over with Nonna to spend part of the day with you."

"I hope they don't stay a long time."

Oh, Dino…

Luca darted Gabi a speaking glance, letting her know that Dino adored her and wanted her to himself forever. She got the message. There was nothing she wanted more, too.

The day turned out to be a hard one to get through when it shouldn't have been. Luca's family stayed all day and enjoyed playing with the dog, too. At one point, she went upstairs to get her packing done so she could leave early in the morning.

They all ate dinner in front of the fire in the

living room and listened to Christmas carols. Dino and Luca stretched out on the floor and played with Nero, who stayed by them, soaking up the warmth. This was bliss, except for the fact that Gabi had to go home and make the most important decision of her life.

She finally said good-night to everyone and went upstairs with Dino to put him to bed. Luca said he'd come up later. His son asked her to read *How the Grinch Stole Christmas* to him after he'd said his prayers.

When she'd finished she said, "Don't you love it when the Grinch realized Christmas didn't come from a store? Christmas was in a person's heart, and his grew three sizes that day."

"Can a heart really do that?" Just as Dino asked the question, her telephone rang.

"Yes," his father answered it from the doorway. He'd brought Nero in the crate with him.

She glanced at both of them. "Excuse me. It's my mother. I need to get it. *Buona notte, piccolino.*"

After giving him a kiss on the forehead, Gabi rushed past Luca and hurried to the guest bedroom. For the first time since staying in the villa, she locked the door. It wasn't to keep

Luca out, but to keep her from giving in to temptation when she hadn't made any decision yet.

She called her mother back and said she'd be at the house in the morning before going to work. They'd talk then.

By four o'clock she still hadn't fallen asleep and gave up trying. After getting dressed, she reached for her suitcase and purse and left the villa for her car. This was for the best. Another prolonged goodbye would kill her.

Two and a half hours later after driving on parts of the highway with black ice, she arrived in Padova. Thank heaven her mother was an early riser. After Gabi got home, she didn't have to wait long to hear her mother making coffee in the kitchen.

Gabi ran to her and they hugged.

"What on earth is going on?"

"You won't believe what happened after we took Dino home from the hospital." For the next little while she told her about the events that led up to Dino's entry into her bedroom following his dog. "I about died when he asked if Luca and I were making a baby."

"Oh, no!" Her mother laughed till the tears trickled out of her eyes." Then silence filled the room for a minute. Her mother had sobered. "Tell me what's going on with you."

"Luca has asked me to marry him, but I'm afraid I can't."

"Because Santos proved to be what your father would have called poor protoplasm?"

"He was worse than that, Mamma, but even being the womanizer he was, I couldn't keep him interested."

"Santos married you to make himself look good, but you couldn't have known that at the time. It didn't take long before you found out he'd never intended to be faithful. Apparently he'd had that woman on the side for years, but she wasn't the kind you married."

"But what does that say about me?"

"That the moment you found out he'd been betraying you, my courageous daughter moved out that very day and filed for divorce. Do you know how many thousands, probably millions of women, would have stayed and put up with that in order to have a man take care of her? I was so proud of you, I could have burst!"

Gabi blinked. "I didn't know you felt that way. If you only knew how terrible I felt to intrude on you when you thought I was happily married."

"I was thrilled beyond words you had the gumption and the strength to walk away even if your heart had been ripped out and you felt humiliated. Not every woman is lucky enough to be married to the right man the first time."

"*You* were."

"Your *papà* was a special man. When we lost him, I know you missed him so terribly, it's the reason Santos's interest in you filled the void he left. But only temporarily. I'm glad you found him out so fast. The person who told you about Santos's activities did you the greatest favor of your life."

"I agree."

"Gabi—I know you were very bitter in the beginning, with reason. Since the day you moved back in with me, I've prayed the right man would come along when the time was right. Who would have dreamed it would happen through a precious child needing an operation? I think you were guided to work for Edda."

"That's a beautiful story."

"You need to believe it."

"Last night Luca told me a lot of things about his life I never knew that aren't beautiful. He has a dominating father who has tried to run his life." Gabi told her about Giselle. "Luca said he wouldn't let his father interfere with us, but nothing's that simple."

"I think you're using that as an excuse."

Gabi grabbed hold of a chair back. "Maybe I am. But what if we got married and he finds me lacking once the bloom of the marriage has worn off? There will always be women attracted to him, and some who'll want to do something about it."

Her mother cocked her head. "Santos did a lot more damage to you than I thought. Have you told Luca everything about your marriage?"

"Yes."

"But he has no idea how afraid you are to trust a man again. This is where faith comes into the picture. If you helped Dino believe in a miracle to get through his operation, don't you think you should show the same faith and trust in Luca?

"That little boy's father molded him, and he adores you. So does his father, who needs you to help him raise that child. Do you know if he wants more children?"

She nodded. "He said he did."

They looked at each other for a minute. "Are

you going to say anything to Edda when you go to work this morning?"

"How can I? I don't know my own mind yet."

Her mother finished her coffee. "Don't take too long. There's a child and his father waiting for your answer."

A sad-looking child stared at Luca as they sat having breakfast together. Not even getting a new dog could make a dent in what was wrong. This wasn't the way things were supposed to go after Dino's operation.

"How come Gabi didn't come and say good-bye to me before she left for Padova this morning?"

Luca had to think fast. "She was worried she'd get caught in traffic if she didn't leave early."

"She promised she'd come back. But what if she doesn't?"

His son had just brought up Luca's greatest fear. "We have to give her time to get her work done."

"I want her to help us train Nero."

Luca took a deep breath. "She'll be back soon." While they were in the family room playing with the dog, Ines came in. "Your father is in the living room."

Luca patted Dino's shoulder. "I have to talk to your *nonno* for a minute. I'll be right back."

He walked through the house to the front room, where his father stood in front of the fire. Naturally he hadn't come to see Dino. "Papà?"

"Good. You're here. Now that Dino is out of the woods, I thought we'd make our announcement together."

"What announcement? I thought you were supposed to be taking things easy."

"I'm much better. The doctor says I can go back to work full-time now as long as you and I share the CEO job."

That was news to Luca, who couldn't imagine anything worse. He didn't have to guess why this had happened the minute the operation was over. Luca hadn't been wrong when he'd told Gabi that his father wasn't through running his life.

"Before you say anything, I want you to know that Giselle and her father will be having dinner with your mother and me at home this evening. I expect you to be there. Leave Dino at home with Ines. This is for business."

More than ever he understood why Gabi had been so alarmed after having been left to deal with his father in the hospital room.

Luca fought down his anger. "You'll have to have dinner without me. End of discussion. Please leave, Papà. You know the way out." He stared at him until the older man left the room and slammed the front door on his way out.

CHAPTER TEN

"HERE'S THE FRIDAY bundle of letters." Stefania passed them around the conference table at the foundation. The whole place was lit up like a Christmas tree. But Gabi had been in such a bad way since returning to Padova, she couldn't get into the spirit of the holiday.

There'd been no word from Luca, or emails from Dino. Why would there be when she'd told Luca she wasn't ready to give him an answer yet?

Work should be saving her life, but nothing was helping her. She started opening the letters, but for once she couldn't concentrate. Before long the women took turns reading. When it came to Clara's turn, she read, "My name is Dino Berettini and I'm seven years old."

Gabi gasped out loud and almost fell out of the chair.

"I'm all better from my operation."

She'd already told her coworkers the marvelous news on Wednesday morning when she'd reported for work. Everyone smiled and looked at Gabi.

"Now I wish Gabi would be my new *mamma*. I love and miss her. So does my new dog, Nero, and my *papà*. He still isn't happy."

Gabi shot to her feet. She remembered what Giustina had said about Dino. He was an angel and an imp.

The little imp in him had found a way to get to her heart. Was it Luca or his *nonna* who'd mailed the letter? It had to have been mailed the very day she'd come back to Padova. Realizing Dino had printed those words himself, she knew *her* heart had already grown three sizes, big enough to blot out past fears forever.

"Forgive me, everyone, but I need to talk to Edda."

Clara got up and handed her the letter. After giving her a hug, they all clapped and wished her *buon Natale*.

Edda read the letter and asked Gabi what she was waiting for. "I expect to be invited to the wedding!"

Gabi flew home, threw some clothes in her suitcase and drove to Maniago at full speed beneath a semisunny sky. On the way, she phoned her mother, who was at work, and told her another miracle had happened. She'd be in touch.

After reaching the villa, she hurried up to the front door and knocked. Her heart was pounding so hard, she was almost ill with excitement.

"Ah," Ines cried when she opened the door and saw her.

Gabi put her finger to her own lips. "Is Dino here? I want to surprise him." The older woman nodded. "He's in the family room with his *papà*."

"Thank you."

When she dashed through the house and entered the room, the first thing she saw was Dino seated at the table putting a puzzle together. As she got closer, the dog yapped. Dino raised his dark head.

"*Gabi*—" In the next instant he'd reached her and flung his arms around her waist. She hugged him hard.

"We got your letter this morning at the Start with a Wish foundation."

He threw his head back. "You did?"

"Yes, and as soon as I read it, I said goodbye to Edda and drove straight here to tell you I want to be your new *mamma* more than anything in the world."

She felt a pair of strong male arms enfold both of them. "What took you so long, *bellissima*?" Luca whispered against her neck. He must have been over in the corner taking care of Nero. "Don't ever do this to me again. I couldn't take it."

Christmas Eve had finally arrived. Their wedding day.

"Dino? We need to leave for Padova. What are you doing?"

"I'm coming. I had to go to the bathroom." He came running to the foyer. "I hope Nero will be okay at Paolo's house."

"For one night he'll be fine."

Ines had helped him dress in a new navy blue suit. Luca had also purchased a formal midnight-blue suit for the wedding. They both wore spotless white shirts and lighter blue ties.

"You both look splendid," Giustina commented.

Luca thought his mother looked lovely in a champagne-colored suit and told her so. The three of them hurried out to the car for the drive to Limena.

Maria and Tomaso were bringing Ines and Pia in their car. They would be congregating at the elegant, private, nineteenth-century villa located in the heart of Limena for the 10:00 p.m. ceremony. Once the priest married them, they'd proceed to the Valbrenta hotel for dinner and an overnight. Christmas morning they'd drive back to Maniago and spend all day at the villa celebrating.

Luca promised Gabi to get there in plenty of time while she dealt with the final arrangements. They'd both wanted something small and private with only immediate family. All their friends would celebrate with them at the hotel.

When he reached the villa, he drove around the side to park. They went inside to the foyer, where Luca kissed his mother and left Dino with her. Between the red flowers and Christmas candles, plus the greenery, everything looked out of this world.

"I'll see you in a few minutes, *figlio mio*."

His son beamed before he hurried to a room that would lead into the living room for the ceremony. In a minute Tomaso joined him. The absence of Luca's father was glaringly obvious, but Luca had known he wouldn't be coming.

Tomaso smiled at him as they pinned the red flowers Maria had brought in to attach to their lapels. "My wife and I have fallen in love with Gabi. We know she's going to make you very happy."

"Thanks, Tomaso. Coming from you that means a lot."

"I couldn't imagine happiness two years ago. Now I can't remember what it was like to feel terrible. Dino is a different child. He adores her."

Luca nodded. "She has a way that hooked me within five minutes of meeting her."

A moment later, a villa staff worker summoned them into the living room, where Father Giovanni stood in front of a beautiful stained glass window resplendent in his vestments. Luca couldn't believe the time had finally come. In ways he felt like he'd been marking time forever. Yet it had only been a month.

From the doorway leading in from the foyer he saw Gabi enter. She walked slowly in a cream-colored lace suit and met him in front of the priest. One creamy rose had been tucked in her blond hair. Could a heart fail you? Luca didn't know, but for a moment he couldn't catch his breath at the gorgeous sight of her.

They clasped hands to face the priest.

"Dearly beloved, what a special time this is to repeat vows of love in this holy place filled with the love of our Lord. Tonight we celebrate the time of his birth and rejoice that two hearts are being joined as one. Tonight a third heart also joins us. If Dino Berettini will come forward, please."

Luca was as stunned as Gabi to hear his name said. They both turned to watch his son walk up to them wearing a red flower in his lapel, too. "Dino, if you'll stand at your father's other side."

Dino did his bidding.

"Dino talked to me in private and expressed his desire to be part of this wedding ceremony because he is so happy. Certainly our Lord is happy on this sacred night. Let us pray."

The rest of the ceremony was a blur to Luca, whose heart was so filled with love for this woman and his son, it didn't seem real. They shared a sweet kiss. It had been arranged that Tomaso would hand Luca the simple gold wedding band to put on her finger. But it was Dino who performed the service in a princely manner with a face that glowed.

"...and now I pronounce you Luca Berettini, and you Gabriella Russo, man and wife."

Luca gave Gabi a loving kiss before Dino came around to hug her. The three of them embraced with the man and the boy on either side of her. This was Christmas joy beyond measure for her.

As she looked into Luca's blue eyes, she thought she'd never seen anything so beautiful. They were a real family now. She could feel his love.

Then she turned her head and stared down into Dino's blue eyes, alive with light. Gabi felt overwhelmed by love for her own little boy who had the most amazing personality. When he wanted something with all his heart, he didn't let anything stop him. Who else but Dino would have asked for such a favor from the priest? This wedding ceremony would be remembered forever.

Once they reached the foyer, Gabi was hugged by her mother, then Luca's mother and the Guardinos. Luca finally caught her around the waist and ushered her through the villa to the car. They left for the hotel and the celebrating.

"Ooh," Dino said while his blue eyes took in everything.

"It's so beautiful," Gabi exclaimed!

"Not as exquisite as my new wife." Luca gave her a husband's kiss in front of everyone.

The hotel had gone all out for their wedding. Besides dozens of Christmas trees with white lights, they'd twined glittering white wedding bells among the Christmas greenery. With white candles lighting every table in the dining room, Gabi couldn't believe it was real.

Besides fish, they were served *agnolotti* and gnocchi, more pasta stuffed with ricotta and spinach, potatoes and pumpkin covered in butter and sage sauce. For dessert, panettone, Dino's favorite Christmas bread. The eating didn't stop until Luca slid a possessive arm around her hip, reminding her of the wedding night to come.

Outside the hotel, church bells were ringing all over the city. "It's the midnight hour. *Buon Natale*, Signora Berettini."

Christmas *had* come, and with it a new life for the three of them.

Gabi kissed Dino good-night, then her

mother, who was keeping him with her for the night.

"Everyone has been taken care of," Luca whispered against her ear. "Now it's time to take you to bed, something I've been wanting to do forever."

"You think I haven't wanted the same thing?" Her legs shook like jelly as he helped her out of the dining room to the elevator of the hotel. Luca had booked the bridal suite, but she hardly noticed it because he carried her over the threshold to the bedroom.

They fell into each other's arms, consumed by the need to pour out their love and forget the world. "*Ti adoro, mia moglie.* Love me, Gabi," he cried. "Love me and never, ever let me go."

CHAPTER ELEVEN

DINO'S EIGHTH BIRTHDAY party fell on December twenty-third. The festivities were in full gear in the family room of the villa when Gabi started to feel pains in her lower back.

At first she thought it was because she'd been doing a lot of work and was just tired. But no matter how she moved or sat, the pain wouldn't go away, and it was getting worse with stinging sensations. These had to be labor pains.

They'd invited Dino's school class. Paolo's mother, Bianca, had been helping her along with Ines and Luca's mother. Bianca's baby was now six months old, and Bianca looked in fabulous shape already.

Gabi felt like a walrus even though Luca told her she'd never been more beautiful. She walked over to Bianca to tell her she needed to visit the bathroom and got there barely in time before her water broke.

In another minute she reached the kitchen. The clock said four thirty. "Pia? Will you call my husband? He's in the study. I'm in labor. He needs to drive me to the hospital."

"Aiee!" She picked up the phone while Gabi stood there in shock, clinging to the counter. Their baby was coming. They'd found out it was a girl, and no one had been more excited and attentive than Luca.

"Tesoro?"

She could hear her husband's voice as he ran down the hall and burst into the kitchen.

"It's really coming?"

"Yes! My water just broke. Will you grab my overnight bag in the bedroom? I'll meet you at the car."

What a far cry from the last time she was in a hospital with Dino. This time Luca helped her inside the ER, and she was immediately wheeled up to the maternity ward. She was taken into her own labor room where Luca could be with her the whole time.

His face had a slight pallor. It had been so long since he'd been worried about anything, she felt terrible for him. But there wasn't anything she could do about it. Her pains were coming hard and consistently.

She was checked several times but told that a first baby took its time. When she saw that it had gotten to be 10:00 p.m., the anesthesiologist came in and gave her an epidural. It helped the pain, but the baby still wasn't ready.

Luca held her hand, looking like death. He finally got up and said he was going to find a doctor. In a way she was glad he left the room. When he came back gowned with a mask, another doctor was with him. He did a check.

"It's still going to be a while. Your obstetrician will be here when you're ready, so don't worry."

"He should be here now," Luca muttered after the resident left. "I wish I could do something for you. I've never felt so helpless in my life."

"You've done enough by getting me in this condition," she teased him, but her joke didn't go over. "Now it's up to me."

Finally, her obstetrician came in at five after twelve, gowned and masked. "Let's have a baby, shall we, Signora Berettini?"

"Please," Gabi half cried. She was exhausted.

"Do you realize it's December twenty-fourth? This little one is a Christmas Eve baby. That's a special blessing. Luca? You sit by her head while I do the rest. Now that you've put on gloves, don't touch anything."

"Can you believe it's finally happening?" she cried to her husband.

The pediatrician and two medical staff members came in to get things ready. She kept her eyes on Luca. He was her rock, her lover, her life! "Remember where we were a year ago tonight?"

"As if I could ever forget our wedding, *innamorata*."

"The head is coming. Bear down again, Gabi. Everything looks good." Before long they both heard a gurgle and the baby emerged. "That's a fine, lusty cry," the doctor said.

"Our baby girl—" Tears trickled from her eyes.

"Here she is, Mamma." The doctor put her on Gabi's stomach. "Luca? Come around to this side and you can cut the cord. Your first job as her *papà*."

Gabi started crying as she looked at the baby. "She's gorgeous!"

"She's just like you with a dusting of golden hair," Luca exclaimed.

After he'd cut the cord, the pediatrician took the baby to weigh and check. "Three point one-eight kilograms, fifty point eight centimeters," he called out. "Her breathing is excellent. She looks perfect. *Complimenti!*"

The nurse cleaned her and wrapped her up before bringing her over to Gabi, who was dying to hold her.

"Oh, darling—can you stand it? We've got our little girl."

Luca's color had returned. He took his time examining every inch of her. First he'd kiss her, then he'd kiss Gabi.

The doctor smiled at them. "She's a beauty. What are you going to name her?"

"We're still debating. We all have a favorite, but it's going to be a family decision as soon as our son gets here."

No sooner had the doctor left than the room started to fill with all the relatives, including Gabi's mother. But it was Dino who beat everyone and came running over to them.

"Here's your new sister, Dino. What do you think of her?"

He got up close to her and studied her for a long time. "She looks kind of funny."

Luca put his arm around him. "You should have seen what you looked like when you were first born."

Dino giggled. "Where's her hair?"

"There's a little bit there, *figlio mio*. It'll all come in soon."

"Her eyes look kind of muddy."

"They'll probably turn green or blue," Luca explained. "We'll have to wait and see."

How she loved this son of theirs. "Do you think she looks like an Alessandra?"

He made a face. "No."

"How about Elana?" Luca said.

"Hmm, no. Can we call her Daniela?"

Gabi eyed her husband. "What do you think about that name?"

"I like it. What made you think of it?"

"She's in one of my favorite cartoons."

"It's a good thing she's not a boy or you'd probably want to name him *Diabolik*," Gabi teased.

Everyone laughed, Luca loudest of all. He turned around to talk to the family. "It's official. Meet the latest addition to our family. Daniela Berettini."

Carefully he passed the baby around so everyone could hold her. While they were all engrossed, someone else entered the room. *Luca's father.* Gabi couldn't believe it.

He looked at Luca. "Please may I come in,

son? I missed Dino's delivery. I didn't want to miss this one."

Gabi locked eyes with Giustina. The two of them realized this was a turning point for better relations between Luca and his father. "Why don't you hand the baby to him?" she whispered.

Giustina lifted the precious bundle and showed him their new granddaughter. He studied her for a moment before kissing her head. "She's beautiful, just like her *mamma*."

With those words Gabi knew this was the closest thing to an olive branch they'd ever receive from the older man. She smiled up at the misty-eyed husband she adored. "Our Christmas Eve baby really is a blessing."

While everyone continued to marvel over Daniela, Luca leaned over to hug her to him the best way he could. He didn't have to say a word, but she knew. No matter how terribly his father had hurt him, he'd never wanted their estrangement. Thank heaven it was over.

"*Ti amo*, Luca. I love our new baby. I love Dino. I love you."

She felt his tears drip down her neck. Nothing could have felt more wonderful or healing.

* * * * *

If you enjoyed this story, check out these other great reads from Rebecca Winters

WHISKED AWAY BY HER SICILIAN BOSS
BOUND TO HER GREEK BILLIONAIRE
RETURN OF HER ITALIAN DUKE
THE BILLIONAIRE'S PRIZE

All available now!